MW00945684

WHEN MORNING COMES

by Patricia Calvert

HADDER MACCOLL

THE HOUR OF THE WOLF

THE MONEY CREEK MARE

THE SNOWBIRD

THE STONE PONY

STRANGER, YOU AND I

YESTERDAY'S DAUGHTER

WHEN
MORNING
COMES

PATRICIA CALVERT

CHARLES SCRIBNER'S SONS
NEW YORK

Charles Scribner's Sons Books for Young Readers
Macmillan Publishing Company
866 Third Avenue, New York, NY 10022
Collier Macmillan Canada, Inc.

Printed in the United States of America
First Edition   10 9 8 7 6 5 4 3 2 1

Library of Congress Cataloging-in-Publication Data
Calvert, Patricia.
When morning comes/Patricia Calvert.—1st ed.
p.   cm.
Summary: Fifteen-year-old Cat Kincaid, having failed to fit into a se-
ries of foster homes and finding herself stuck on a farm with an elderly
female beekeeper, secretly longs for a place to be herself, not somebody she has invented.
[1. Foster home care—Fiction.   2. Bee culture—Fiction.
3. Self-acceptance—Fiction.]   I. Title.
PZ7.C139Wh   1989   [Fic]—dc19   89–5854   CIP   AC
ISBN 0-684-19105-9

Dedicated with affection to
Mary Schwager,
Dorothy Tienter,
and Renée Van Vleet

1

"I suppose you know as well as I do what's going to happen if things don't work out this time," Mrs. Allen warned.

Cat resolutely kept her gaze fastened on the highway and pretended to ignore the remark. There was more to come; Mrs. Allen was never content with one comment if she thought a dozen might make a deeper impression.

"The department regulations are quite specific about three placements being the maximum," she went on, true to form. "I tried to be so careful about explaining that to you in our very first interview, remember? I had hoped, you see, that if you fully understood our policies, you would be more prudent in your behavior."

Mrs. Allen hunched forward, blue eyes squinty behind the lenses of her silver-rimmed glasses, bony hands clamped onto the steering wheel with a white-knuckled grip. Cat studied the social worker suspiciously from the corner of her eye. The old witch was even more uptight

1

than usual this afternoon. So what was the big problem? Didn't she know how to get to this new place, or had she already decided that a third placement would probably end as badly as the first two?

Cat yawned pointedly to make it plain to Mrs. Allen that she personally didn't care diddly whether she was placed again, or where, or with whom. She turned, bored, and stared sullenly out the car window. Tall weeds grew thickly near the edge of the road, and since Mrs. Allen's car was one of those dinky foreign jobs, some of the weeds were nearly as tall as the car itself.

"Did you hear what I just said, Cathleen?" Mrs. Allen inquired testily, her voice rising an octave.

Call me Cat! Cat wanted to yell at her. Was the old bag deaf or just plain stubborn? I'm Cat now, she had explained right at the beginning; that's who I've been for almost a year. The person Mrs. Allen insisted on referring to, someone named Cathleen Kincaid, was dead and gone, not that anyone really missed her, including Gwendolyn C. Kincaid, mother of the not-so-recently deceased.

"Yeah, yeah, I heard you already," Cat growled ominously. She'd known Mrs. Allen for about nine months, ever since that first shoplifting charge at the Lakeside Mall. Their acquaintance had lasted long enough, Cat decided, to have deteriorated into an irritable familiarity, a manner of reacting to each other that probably was fairly normal between an aging county social worker who used too much blue rinse in her hair and a street person who'd vowed to take charge of her own life.

It was a relationship that could be greatly improved, however, by one small, simple admission on the part of Mrs. Allen. "Call me Cat," Cat requested softly for the umpteenth time. After all, hadn't she become a person

2

who lived by her wits, who walked alone? Yes, she had; she was like a cat now, always on the move; she was a stalker, a predator, not anybody's prey.

"My name's Cat now," she insisted evenly, "so you might as well get used to it. No way are you welfare freaks gonna change me back into the person I used to be."

2

The trouble with Mrs. Allen, Cat would have been willing to explain if anyone had wanted to listen, was that the old bat was just too old to be a good social worker. She was one of those scrawny, determined do-gooders who unfortunately didn't want to hear certain things. Her own youth was so far behind her that it had to have been part of the Dark Ages. In Cat's opinion, she'd have done everybody a big favor by retiring twenty years ago.

Whenever Cat tried to describe what life on the street was like, for instance, or when she talked about the stuff that went on down at the Hideout, poor Mrs. Allen's eyes got a glazed look behind the lenses of her glasses, and she'd begin to chew on her lower lip as if she were afraid she might hear other things she didn't want to know. Cat had always been sorry she hadn't gotten a case worker like Floss's, a guy who'd just gotten out of college and was on his first job. Guys were easier to handle; you could always hustle a guy, but a woman could be so hard-nosed, especially if she was the skinny type with a chicken neck and blue hair.

The old ditz sure knew how to lecture, though, and Cat suspected that's what she was in for next. Mrs. Allen had a large, dull inventory of you-know-what'll-happen-if-you-don't-shape-up sermons, and she could give one at the drop of a hat. Yawn, yawn. Cat slouched deeper into her seat, closed her eyes, and waited for the inevitable. As expected, Mrs. Allen didn't disappoint her.

"Let me tell you, if you pull any more stunts like you did a few months ago at the Wilsons'," the social worker intoned, "not to mention the bad time you gave the Turners, then I can promise you that your next stop will be the girls' home at Ellensburg, Cathleen."

She managed to get everything right except my name, Cat mused bitterly behind closed eyes. "Your habit of acting out your problems is going to catch up with you eventually, you know," Mrs. Allen cautioned.

Blah, blah, blah; acting out was one of Mrs. Allen's favorite subjects. She'd explained once what it meant; supposedly it was when a person did impulsive things rather than face what the real problem was. "Stick it, lady," Cat had retorted. "If it's all the same to you, *I'll* decide what my real problem is."

Mrs. Allen hesitated in midsermon and slowed her car briefly. Cat opened one eye, just wide enough to see her peer with increasing anxiety toward the left side of the road as if she were searching for an unfamiliar exit.

"On the other hand," Mrs. Allen went on, speeding up again and turning her attention back to the highway, "if you could make it through the summer with Miss Bowen, there might be a good chance that we'd agree to let you stay with her. You could forget what happened this past year, and just because you dropped out of school last semester doesn't mean that you can't ever go back again. We could arrange to have your records transferred to this school district; you're a bright girl, and you'd catch up quickly."

Cat knew from the tone of Mrs. Allen's voice that she was warming up to her sermon and would soon get to one of her favorite parts. "And you could put down roots, Cathleen! Roots are so important; they could make putting your life back together so much easier."

"Roots are for trees," Cat hissed under her breath. Mrs. Allen was big on roots and preached about them every chance she got, nearly as often as she talked about putting your life back together. Before a person got on anybody else's case about putting a life back together, though, both parties ought to agree that it was broken. That was one more subject on which she and Mrs. Allen did not see eye to eye.

Mrs. Allen and the rest of those welfare freaks down at the county offices were wrong about something else too: the threat about getting shipped off to the girls' home in Ellensburg didn't sound as horrible as they thought it did. At a place like that, Cat reflected, there'd be lots of girls like herself, a fact that made being sent there seem almost as cool as going off to summer camp probably seemed to a rich kid.

Girls who ended up at Ellensburg would be the kind who'd been screwed up, Cat reasoned, eyes still clamped shut. They'd be girls who'd been dumped by their folks or who'd been abused or who'd just plain run off, as she'd done herself, with a vow never to return to what had been left behind.

Women like Mrs. Allen, of course, had the weird idea

that if you were on the street, it was because somebody had put you there. No matter how often you explained yourself to these welfare types, they couldn't get it through their thick heads that a person might actually choose to be on the street, that it might be a better place to be than the one you'd come from.

Cat decided that she wouldn't try to explain herself again. She groaned mightily, sat up, hauled her purse off the floor of Mrs. Allen's car, and, bored out of her gourd, began to paw through its jumbled contents.

"Miss Bowen—I guess everyone calls her Annie—has been working off and on with our department for several years," Mrs. Allen rattled on. She braked suddenly for a turnoff, casting herself and Cat hard against their seat belts, decided at the last moment that it still wasn't the right one, and nervously speeded up again. Cat tried to shut her ears to the social worker's words and continued to grub through her purse.

"So I was pleased that when I called her a couple of days ago and told her about you, she agreed that I could bring you down this afternoon. She told me that she had an awfully busy summer planned but that she'd be glad to help us out—and you too, of course."

Of course, Cat mimicked soundlessly and plucked a mirror with a pink plastic handle from the depths of her handbag. It was the one she'd shoplifted from Woolworth's when she lived with the Wilsons. She held it up and studied the face that stared back at her.

No zits. Wasn't it incredible? Most girls her age had so many, had to use gunk in tubes and bottles to keep 'em covered up, but she only got one once in a while. It was probably one of the things that made her look older than fifteen, plus of course the fact that she had a body that looked almost like a grown woman's. Along with hardly ever getting a zit, she'd gone from being a skinny twelve-year-old to being practically grown up without having to suffer through the knobby, lanky look that came in between.

Pleased with her reflection in the mirror, Cat nevertheless stroked on fresh iridescent violet eye shadow (Summer Storm, her favorite color) and considered touching up her eyeliner. Better not, she decided; the way old lady Allen was cruising down the pike this afternoon, she might end up putting out an eye.

"And I'm sure you're going to really like Miss Bowen—Annie, I mean," Mrs. Allen declared fervently. "All the reports I've heard about her are so positive. Our other girls apparently got to be very fond of her."

"I, my dear lady, am not just another one of your girls," Cat considered informing Mrs. Allen, "and most likely I will despise her on sight. Remember how I didn't get on with those neatniks in that first foster home you stuck me in?" The place had smelled strongly of lemon wax; you had to leave your shoes at the back door; the supper dishes were whisked off the table and into the dishwasher almost before you'd finished eating. She'd only lasted four days there; she'd been as happy to leave as the family had been to get rid of her. The welfare department decided not to count it as one of the three placements; they called it a bad fit instead.

Tell me about it, Cat thought bitterly, and smoothed some blusher (Egyptian Plum) on her cheeks. Next, she polished her lips with colorless gloss, then examined her reflection a second time.

A pair of green eyes flecked with gold, fringed with sooty lashes and ringed with smudged day-old black eyeliner stared back at her. Her hair, black as a crow's wing (she'd done the dye job just before running away from the Turners') hung in tangled corkscrews to her shoulders. Her mouth, gleaming lips held slightly apart, turned neither up nor down. Cat sighed, satisfied with what she saw. It was true, she admitted privately; she actually *did* look like a cat.

Until that afternoon under the bridge near Lawrie Park, she'd never thought much about whether she looked like a cat or a dog or somebody's pet canary. It had been someone else, a stranger, who had pointed out to her the essence of her own true nature. That might not have happened if she hadn't skipped her last two classes at Jefferson that day; having gotten a D on that history exam had made the rest of the afternoon seem pretty pointless and had been the only excuse she'd needed to take off for the Hideout.

High above the Lawrie River, where the Harley Street bridge intersected with the riverbank, a cavelike hole, left during construction of the bridge, had over time been hollowed out even further by a variety of down-and-out tenants. It'd been furnished with broken lawn chairs, an old couch, a couple of ottomans with the stuffing sprouting through their plastic upholstery, end tables made out of packing crates. When it rained, you never got wet at the Hideout, and after a while you even got used to the steady drumming of traffic far above your head.

The best thing about the Hideout was that anytime you went down there somebody was always hanging out. Mostly it was dudes from the street, but lots of times chicks showed up too. On the afternoon after the D in history, the guys were all drinking Colt 45, and a voice had cried above the din of traffic, "Hey, woman! What'd you do to your hair?"

Cat remembered peering through the mellow gloom cast by the concrete bridge pillars but hadn't been able to tell for sure who had spoken. "You remind me of a cat, babe," someone else called out. Had it been the cool guy named Rambo or that older, nerdy character called Duke?

"Yeah, you do!" he'd called out enthusiastically. "You're like one of them big black cats in the jungle, all cool and calculating. I got a feeling you're one of them no-heart women, the kind who takes what she wants and leaves a guy with a broken heart." It had sounded kind of neat, Cat remembered. Those guys had been boozing it up all afternoon, though, and smoking God-only-knew-what, which probably had a lot to do with their opinions.

Later, however, when Cat got back to Davey Gibson's apartment upstairs over the Used Goods Galore store on Harley Street, there'd been a program on the tube that was all about jungle animals, cats in particular. A leopard had stalked across the screen, green-eyed and dangerous, and Cat had been amazed to realize, Yes, that's what I am, a cat. . . .

There were all types of jungles, she had reasoned. There was the leafy green kind filled with screaming parrots and flowers in colors from a psychedelic nightmare, and then there was the asphalt-and-concrete kind, where a blade of grass wouldn't grow if you prayed over it. In either kind of jungle, though, being a predatory loner meant you weren't a victim yourself, right? On that afternoon, sitting alone in front of Davey's TV, she'd christened herself Cat Kincaid. She'd gotten a second beer out of Davey's fridge, had silently toasted the demise of the girl she used to be, and baptized the new one.

Cat yawned, grateful that Mrs. Allen had kept her mouth shut for a few minutes, and dropped the mirror back into her purse. Once you'd made up your mind to take care of yourself, though, it sure was a drag to be made into somebody's project just because the welfare department kept interfering. Now, for the third time, she was about to be rescued, Cat mused, even though she'd never once hollered for help.

This time, she was going to get saved by a person named Annie Bowen, who apparently had a hobby of helping delinquent girls. Jeez! People like her ought to make donations to the Save the Children Fund and leave me alone, Cat thought resentfully. If that dude under the bridge had been able to see that she was able to take care of herself, why didn't the welfare creeps see it too and just bug off?

Something else too: I *like* Harley Street, Cat protested silently to her reflection in the window of Mrs. Allen's car. No way did being on the street mean that a person was lonely. Hey, far from it. Anyway, it was a gas to be on the move all the time, to crash someplace different almost every night—one night at Josie's, who'd dropped out of Jefferson two years ago, then a couple of nights at Davey's pad, finally a night or two with Floss and with Angie. Floss had a kid now, though; its nose ran all the time and it cried a lot, which was a real bummer. Then, after you'd done musical beds you started the cycle all over again, which meant you hardly ever had to spend a night at home.

Home. Cat squinted against the highway glare. The word sounded funny; it was round and soft and whole, the way home hadn't been for a long time.

Once, before she'd gotten the hang of making it on the

street, Cat spent a night in Lawrie Park. That turned out to be a real dicey thing to do; she'd waked up to discover strange hands exploring her body, fumbling at the waistband of her jeans. Jeez! She'd jerked a knee up hard where it'd do the most damage, had jumped up and run fast toward the lights on the bridge, leaving someone bent over double and cursing in the shrubs beside the joggers' path. Listen, it was one thing to get it on with a guy because you liked him, but jungle law number one ought to be Thou Shalt Not Jump a Person's Bones Without Permission. Not that the experience had made her want to go home again.

"So how much longer is it gonna take to get where we're going?" Cat groaned. They'd been driving for more than an hour, getting farther and farther from the park, the bridge, Harley Street, everything that was familiar, a fact that was beginning to get on her nerves. The ride had been duller than it needed to be too because Mrs. Allen refused to tune in to the rock station and wouldn't even put on that Bon Jovi tape that Cat had taken from Davey's place before she left. She wondered idly if he'd be mad when he missed it. He was pretty cool about stuff like that, though; Davey did drugs a lot now and was mellow almost all the time.

"I'm not exactly sure," Mrs. Allen admitted. She had chewed persistently on her lower lip, and now a raw pink edge showed there. "According to the directions they gave me at the office, I had expected we'd be there by now."

Cat slumped back down in her seat. "What's the name of this burg where I'll be staying?" she wanted to know, and glanced down to admire the red sequin rose stitched on the left side of her black T-shirt.

The shirt fit like a second skin, and her jeans were her favorite pair, the black ones with the silver rivets in the shape of stars. She'd lifted them out of the Sears store a few months ago. The jeans had been pretty tight to start with; now, after several washings, they were almost too tight to sit down in comfortably. She'd wanted to look spectacular today, though, just in case old lady Allen stopped for gas somewhere. Gas stations were good places to hit on guys; if she met anybody she liked, maybe she'd let him know where she was headed. Sometime she might be able to meet him when he got off work.

Cat prayed silently that the new town wouldn't be too small. With luck, it would at least have a pizza joint or a video arcade to hang out at. She'd almost lost her marbles in that burg last summer. What was its name? Yeah; Rosemont. Pittsville was more like it.

"A wonderful place to raise a family," the Wilsons had boasted proudly. "Terrific," Cat remembered sneering, "so how about raising a dozen of your own and leaving me where I belong?" The main street in Rosemont had been a measly two blocks long. A big night turned out to be hanging out in front of the Supersave, hoping some cute guy might cruise past.

"Ummmm," Mrs. Allen murmured, her attention fastened on the left side of the highway. "They told me at the office that Annie Bowen lives on a farm."

Cat shot bolt upright in her seat. "A *what?*" she screeched. "Nobody told *me* anything about any farm!" She glared in stunned disbelief at the highway, then back at Mrs. Allen. "No way is this chick into farms," she warned ominously, "and if you welfare creeps think you can make me stay any place that I don't want—"

Mrs. Allen slowed her car and pulled off the highway

13

onto the soft shoulder. She shut off the ignition and, wiggling against the constraint of her safety harness, faced Cat.

"Now you listen to me, Cathleen Kincaid, and you listen to me good," she commanded. Her voice was even sterner than usual, and the blue eyes behind her silver-rimmed glasses were steely with determination. "There's no point whatsoever in either of us finishing this trip if you're going to threaten to leave this new home even before we've gotten there."

Cat was too dazed to be ticked off at Mrs. Allen's no-nonsense tone. A farm, for God's sake! What did those welfare workers do all day? Sit around, drink coffee, and calculate new ways to make other people crazy? What if what they were plotting to do to her was against the law? If she found out it was, Cat vowed, she'd sue! For fifteen million dollars! Didn't they realize she'd never been farther from the city than the Apple Valley Zoo?

"The decision to place you with Annie Bowen was not an accident," Mrs. Allen explained. "Everyone in the department agreed that what you need, Cathleen, is a totally different environment. You see, Harley Street—not to mention those awful people who hang around the park and the things that go on under that bridge—well, in an atmosphere like that, Cathleen, there's no way you can ever get your head straight."

Mrs. Allen could make old-fashioned judgments about the people who hung out in the park, Cat noticed, but in her next breath use a trendy phrase like get your head straight.

"And I meant what I said when we left the city this afternoon," the social worker reminded her. "Either this works out or you're on your way to the detention center at

Ellensburg for sure." Mrs. Allen paused, the harness across her narrow chest making her momentarily short of breath.

"So you must give me your word right now, Cathleen, that you'll give this new place a fair chance," the social worker insisted. "If you aren't able to do that, we might as well head back to the city right now. I'll get started on the paperwork that will be needed to transfer you to—"

"So what kind of a farm is it?" Cat demanded bitterly, as if Mrs. Allen's reply would determine whether or not she'd agree to stay. Cat crossed her arms over her chest, crushing the rose petals on her T-shirt, and was surprised how cool she felt. She glared at the weeds at the edge of the road. A sparrow clung to a nearby stalk and stared perkily back at her. Cat pressed her tongue hard against the window glass, and the startled bird flew off.

"Well?" she demanded. "So what's this stupid farm going to be like?" Would there be horses and pigs and cows? Dogs, cats, chickens? If she could learn to ride horseback, it might not be so bad. She'd already made up her mind, though, not to learn how to milk a cow. The idea of grabbing onto those rubbery pink gizmos under a cow's belly with her bare hands was enough to give her goose pimples all over.

"I don't actually know what kind of farm it is," Mrs. Allen confessed. "Everybody in the department was so high on Miss Bowen that it didn't seem important to ask. As far as I'm concerned, a farm's a farm." Oh, sure, Cat objected silently, but nobody's hauling you out to the boonies to live on one, either.

"Now are you ready to give me your pledge that you'll give Miss Bowen and her farm a fair trial?" Mrs. Allen

15

persisted. "Or should I turn the car around right now and—"

"Okay, okay!" Cat hissed. If it didn't work out—and of course it wouldn't—she could always run away again. So what if they caught up with her eventually and sentenced her to that detention center? The truth was, she wouldn't be eighteen for two-and-a-half more years; only then could she call all her own shots, decide how she wanted to live, where, and with whom. Right now, let's face it, she was s-t-u-c-k.

Well, maybe there'd be a cute dude living on the farm next to the one where she was going to get dumped this afternoon, Cat speculated grimly. Maybe he'd have a motorcycle. It'd only take a couple days to get it on with him; after a week she'd talk him into running away with her. They'd travel mostly at night, would sleep during the day under bridges or in patches of woods along the way. They'd shoplift wieners and buns and beer out of 7-Eleven stores as they headed south, would be careful to keep one jump ahead of the cops until they got all the way to Florida.

Cat smiled dreamily at her smudged reflection in the car window. When they got to the ocean, she'd run right down to the water's edge. She'd jump in and swim until she got to a tiny green island in the middle of all that blue sea. She and Mr. Motorcycle would build themselves a shelter of palm fronds, would go naked like those kids did in *Island of the Blue Dolphins*. They'd bake turtle eggs in a fire pit on the beach, drink fresh coconut milk, and nobody would ever hassle them again. . . .

Mrs. Allen started her car and pulled back onto the highway. For fifteen minutes Cat rode beside her in stony silence. Then the social worker gave a rusty sigh of relief, crossed a railroad track, and turned onto a narrow road framed by alternate rows of pines and poplars. On the passenger's side of the car near the turnoff was a weathered yellow sign partly hidden by wild grapevine and painted with chipped black letters.

SWEETBERRY BEE FARM, Cat read through the foggy smudge left by her wet tongue, Home of the Sweetest Taste This Side of Paradise.

"A bee farm!" she howled, freshly outraged. "Nobody with an IQ of ten would take a street kid like me out to the sticks to live on a bug farm!" she protested furiously. "You can't be serious about—"

"Bees are not bugs," Mrs. Allen interrupted wearily. "I mean, they're not ordinary bugs. They work; they make honey. I suppose that's how Miss Bowen makes her living—she sells the honey that her bees make. And remember, Cathleen, you gave me your pledge that you'd give this place a fair try."

Cat tilted her head against the headrest and studied the narrow gravel road through slitted green eyes. Sure I did, lady, she admitted silently, but what I never promised you was how long.

3

Cat wondered if Annie Bowen's farmhouse would look like a picture on a calendar. She imagined that it would be painted white; its shutters would be green. The lawn all around it would be as smooth as a piece of velvet, and a pair of oak trees would stand like sentinels in the front yard. Under the kitchen windows there'd be boxes of bushy red geraniums, and a sable-and-white collie dog would stand guard behind a white picket fence.

When Mrs. Allen wheeled her car into the driveway of Sweetberry Bee Farm, Cat revised her scenario. She wasn't really surprised; after all, had anything ever turned out as she hoped it would? Annie's farm was no exception, so scratch the white paint and the green shutters, give up on the lawn that looked like velvet, on the oak trees and the collie. Delete everything except the geraniums.

Annie Bowen's farmhouse turned out to be a somewhat shabby pink bungalow that Cat decided had been built by an amateur carpenter. The glassed-in front porch was lower at one end than the other, and each of its windows started and finished at a noticeably different tilt. The geraniums were red, sure enough, but were too spindly to be pretty and grew in splintered wooden tubs scattered across a lawn that hadn't been mowed all season. No noble collie could be seen, but a scroungy yellow mutt slept soundly near a side door. Three skinny chickens pecked at the dog's empty dish, but the famous Annie Bowen was nowhere to be seen.

"She ought to be expecting us," Mrs. Allen complained, casting a troubled glance around the tacky yard. "I talked to her only this morning, so I'm sure she couldn't have forgotten that we were—"

The social worker climbed out of her car but froze in her tracks when the yellow dog rose up from his place near the side door. Instead of rushing at the car with a snarl, however, he limped on three legs to welcome a tall, stout woman in bib overalls who arrived at a lope, elbows flapping, around the corner of the house.

"Down, Peaches," the woman called soothingly, laying a hand on the dog's head. "Try to behave like a gentleman when we have company." The dog paid no mind to her words but persisted in leaping against the woman's knees, despite the fact that, as Cat could see, he was painfully stiff and lame.

Cat felt the muscles in her jaws tighten into knots as hard as walnuts. Just her luck; Annie Bowen looked like a woman who'd gotten A's in phys ed. Another outdoorsy type, she grieved inwardly. The Wilsons had been nature freaks too; they wanted to go camping or hiking practically every weekend. It had finally gotten so bad that she'd run away just to get a little rest. Even worse, Annie Bowen was old, maybe almost as old as Mrs. Allen.

Annie Bowen stuck her hand out to Mrs. Allen. It was a brown, big-knuckled hand, Cat noticed gloomily, and the beekeeper pumped the social worker's limp white one energetically. "And this is Cathleen Kincaid," Mrs. Allen announced, turning to Cat as soon as she rescued her hand from Annie Bowen's.

"Cat," Cat corrected. "Everybody calls me Cat." It wasn't exactly the truth, of course, but she liked the way it sounded. She wondered if Annie Bowen realized that she was about to take into her home a girl who was as dark and dangerous as a leopard.

"Cat it will be, then," the beekeeper agreed heartily. Her gray-brown hair was parted in the middle and hooked behind her ears; her teeth had gaps between them, and her smile was wide and easy.

Cat did not return the smile; she frowned and narrowed her glance so as not to encourage Annie Bowen in the belief that she'd come to Sweetberry by choice. When the beekeeper extended her large brown hand, Cat let her own dangle at her side. Annie Bowen reached for it anyway; her grip was warm and firm.

"And you can just call me Annie, like everybody else," she said invitingly, then gestured in the dog's direction. "This, of course, is Peaches." She glanced down at him with a rueful grin.

"You might not believe it to look at the old boy now, but once upon a time he was the loveliest pup, as pretty as a bowl of peaches and cream, which is the reason I decided to call him Peaches." The old yellow dog, hearing his name, struggled again to rest his paws against his mistress's knees. Annie smiled, and touched him lightly between his soft ears.

"That was a long time ago," she admitted. "I'm afraid most of his peachy days are behind him now."

I know what she's up to, Cat thought. She's trying to soften me up, trying to make things seem cozy and intimate. Well, Annie Bowen would have to be straightened out quick, before she took too much else for granted. What you had to do, Cat had learned, was to let foster parents know right away that you'd been rescued against your will, that you didn't need them or their help.

"I'm not real big on bugs," she announced stonily, "and that includes bees. If I had to pick a place to get dumped, you better believe a bee farm wouldn't be high on my list."

Annie lifted one shoulder in a philosophic shrug and did not seem to take the news personally. "The bees in my colonies are mostly Italians," she remarked, "which is a very mild strain. You might change your mind about them if you stay at Sweetberry long enough to get acquainted."

Well, at least she's admitting that I probably won't hang around long, Cat thought. "And I don't plan to learn how to milk a cow either," she declared, just in case Annie had any misconceptions on that score. Sometimes you really had to spell things out to a new foster parent.

Annie guffawed, surprised. "That's real good news because I don't have a cow on the place!" Cat frowned harder. One thing she hated was to be made fun of.

Ten minutes later, over glasses of lemonade in Annie's cramped, clean kitchen, Cat listened to the two women talk about some of the girls who'd already stayed at Sweetberry. There had been Eloise, she heard, who had finished her senior year at the nearby high school. Liza had thought it was nifty to take care of the chickens. Betsy had gone back home after six months to live with her folks again but sent a Christmas card every year. Big deal; the conversation was enough to put a person to sleep.

Cat tipped her chair back against the kitchen wall and studied Annie through slitted, calculating eyes. The beekeeper was harder to pin a label on than most of the other foster mothers had been. For starters, she apparently was single. Cat felt a corner of her mouth turn up with a sly smile.

Bet the old gal had never been with a guy in her life, she mused. Annie Bowen had the sex appeal of a pumpkin: look at those chubby cheeks, that gap-toothed smile, that whacked-off gray hair that was as straight as string. If a person wanted to describe an old maid, Annie would sure fit the bill.

Cat took a long, thoughtful swallow of lemonade and let the ice cubes clank noisily against her teeth. I'm gonna be more than this lady can handle, she realized with satisfaction. I'll tell her stories that'll put so much frizz in her hair she'll never need a perm. I'll do it soon too, Cat decided vengefully, and savored what the moment would be like. The stories she'd tell—most of them true—would be the same ones that had so scandalized the Wilsons that, what with the shoplifting and all, they'd called Mrs. Allen and admitted maybe they weren't cut out to be foster parents after all.

"Well, then," Cat heard Mrs. Allen exclaim with relief, "now that everything's been settled, I'd best be on my way back to town and just leave you two to—to . . ." The social worker didn't seem to know exactly how to finish her farewell, Cat noticed.

"To our own devices," Annie finished for her with a

wink in Cat's direction. "Don't worry about us; we'll manage to get to know each other soon enough."

Don't bet on it, Cat wanted to advise her. The beekeeper clearly assumed too much; a moment of reckoning would have to come soon.

Mrs. Allen lurched forward when they all rose from the table, and Cat realized with dismay that the social worker meant to administer a farewell hug. She submitted woodenly to Mrs. Allen's embrace, which fortunately was brief. Was the expression in those pale blue eyes suspiciously tender? Cat wondered, alarmed. Jeez, now that she considered it, Cat realized there'd been a couple of other times that Mrs. Allen had seemed to be on the verge of saying something nice, but hadn't quite been able to get the right words out.

Mercifully, she didn't get them out this time either, but after she finally pulled out of Annie's yard and had vanished down the aisle of pines and poplars in her dinky blue car, Cat was surprised to hear the beekeeper herself give a wistful sigh.

"It sounds simple enough, but it's never quite that easy, is it?" Annie Bowen murmured.

"What isn't?" Cat demanded coldly.

"Oh, you know, for people to get to know each other," Annie answered, her wide, white smile replaced by a sweet, reflective one. "It takes time, I guess, and lots of patience—and maybe good luck thrown in—before any of us can manage it."

Talk about a switcheroo, Cat marveled. The old gal knows this probably isn't going to work out, that we aren't going to learn to like each other no matter how hard we try. Actually, it was a big relief. It meant that when she left in just a couple of days and hitched back to Harley Street, Annie wouldn't die of disappointment or shed tears of grief or anything like that. Because for sure that's how it'd all end up; she'd run away from nearly every place the welfare nuts had stuck her, Cat mused, and Sweetberry Farm wasn't going to be an exception. Leave before you get left was her motto. Dump before you get dumped.

When Annie turned back toward the bungalow, Cat did likewise. The beekeeper hesitated, cocked her head, and pressed an index finger to her chin. "To be honest with you, Cat, it never amounted to much as houses go," she admitted. Once again, her smile was wide and friendly. "All my friends told me that I was just plain crazy to buy it. It used to be the gardener's cottage on a much larger estate," she explained. "Look over there." She gestured to the south, and Cat followed her pointing finger. "That's all that's left of the big house. I've heard that it was a grand place in its day, but over the years it's been vandalized so often that I'm not sure it could be salvaged now." Cat detected a wish-filled note in the beekeeper's voice. "I used to daydream about trying to fix it up sometime," Annie added, "but that's all it ever amounted to—just another daydream."

Cat studied the old house. It was about two blocks from the bungalow and stood in the middle of what once had been a lawn but now was mostly a weed patch. Many of its windows had been broken, giving the place a desperate, eyeless look. Portions of the cream-colored siding had rotted away to show lath and plaster underneath, and the newel posts on the veranda had decayed to splinters. It was like a house in one of those spooky Friday-the-thirteenth murder movies, Cat thought, and made herself

24

a mental note to check it out before she took off for Harley Street.

"When I bought this place, I could only afford to buy three acres, which included both these houses," Annie explained. "That really isn't enough land to raise crops on, so I had to decide how I was going to make a living."

Does she really think I care if she bought three acres or three thousand? Cat asked herself.

"Eventually I decided to keep bees," Annie informed her.

Ho hum. "For bees you need only three acres?" Cat drawled, and yawned pointedly in the beekeeper's face.

"Oh, not even that many," Annie seemed delighted to explain. "You see, I work on the out-apiary system, which means that nearly all of my hives—they're called apiaries—are on other folks' property. I put a few hives here, a few hives there; guess I've got them scattered on ten or twelve different sites in the township." Cat watched the beekeeper's eyes gleam with pleasure as she described how she worked.

"Most of the farmers in this area are truck gardeners, you see. They raise corn, tomatoes, okra, squash, strawberries, and bees are a big help when it comes to pollinating crops like that. The system works out great for everyone—me, my neighbors, my bees," Annie finished, her grin showing the gaps between her teeth.

Oh, terrific, Cat thought, and didn't bother to stifle another gigantic yawn. It was quite possible she might OD on boredom before she succeeded in escaping from Sweetberry. Nevertheless, when Annie beckoned her into the bungalow, Cat followed with a dark scowl. She'd probably have to stay at least one night, she decided, and trailed resignedly down the hallway behind the

25

beekeeper, who stepped through a narrow doorway onto the glassed-in front porch.

"This room will be yours for as long as you want to stay at the farm," Annie announced. "As you can see for yourself, it's not especially fancy, but the windows face the east, and you'll wake up every morning to the smile of old Mr. Sun."

The smile of old Mr. Sun? Pardon me, I think I'm going to throw up, Cat was tempted to remark, and didn't bother to hide her disgust. Didn't Annie realize that corn belonged in a cornfield? Obviously, she also didn't know that real life began at sundown, not sunup. With a stab of homesickness that surprised her with its pain, Cat remembered the neon lights of Harley Street at night, the arcades and the alleys, the deals and dealing. Now, that was real life!

"Come in, come in," Annie urged, and reluctantly Cat stepped across the threshold into the bedroom. There was a small braided rug on the floor and a poster from the Audubon Society thumbtacked on the wall above the bed, which was covered with a patchwork quilt. A basket of dried flowers stood on a night table, and next to it was a lamp that had been made out of an old lantern.

Cat turned her attention quickly to the windows, which were as crooked-looking from inside the room as from the outside. Good, she observed; they were the old-fashioned sash type, easy to raise. The drop to the ground outside couldn't be much more than a couple of feet. Some night—tomorrow night, probably—she'd pry one of them open, would hoist a leg over the sill, and would be off down that road hours before Annie realized she was gone.

"You'll notice there aren't any locks on the doors or windows," Annie murmured with a knowing smile. "If you want to know the truth, I've never even locked Peaches up. I guess he sticks around Sweetberry because he figures it's the place he wants to be."

Lay off, lady, Cat wanted to caution Annie. Instead, she turned slowly, laid a flattened palm on her own thrust-out hip, and gave Annie a flinty look. She wasn't going to stand for any more lectures about choices. Jeez! She'd heard enough on that subject to last a lifetime. She'd gotten at least two from Mrs. Allen, one from that doctor at the People's Free Clinic on Harley Street when she had to be treated for that infection a year ago, and one from Mr. Pratt, a teacher at Jefferson. Never one from Mom, of course; Mom wasn't into choices. Mom was into settling for whatever fate handed to her.

"Hey," Annie exclaimed suddenly and pointed through one of the porch windows. "There goes Hooter Lewis!"

Cat ducked to peek under the window sash. All she could see was a puff of yellowish dust on the road she'd ridden up half an hour ago with Mrs. Allen. A second later she glimpsed what looked like the cab of a battered green truck, a lean brown arm hooked out the open window on the driver's side, and a face that was too far away to tell much about except that it was young. The truck disappeared down the road on its way to somewhere else.

"Hooter Lewis?" Cat echoed speculatively.

"He'll probably be back in the morning," Annie told her. "I'm expecting a delivery of bees, and he's the one who usually brings them out. Hooter's a real sweet kid; sometimes he lends me a hand when I divide my colonies or when the honey flow gets too heavy for me to handle alone. I've known Hooter since he was this high," Annie said, holding a hand level with her knee. "It's hard to believe he's seventeen already."

So Hooter Lewis was seventeen, not to mention sweet. He probably didn't know much about girls, Cat reflected, especially not the street-smart kind. Giving him an education might be a real tickle; at least it'd be worth some good laughs with Floss and Angie when she got back to Harley Street. Cat stretched luxuriously and flexed both arms high over her head. Leopards in the heart of the jungle stretched too, she imagined, as they set off on the trail of fresh prey.

"Hey, the room's okay," she assured Annie. "Let's face it, I've sure slept in a lot worse."

Look, there was no big rush to lift up one of those windows, right? She could leave any time she felt like it; now that she'd heard about Hooter Lewis, though, the prospect of hanging around Sweetberry for a while took on an unexpected appeal. And she might get real lucky. She might be able to talk Hooter Lewis into running off to Florida with her in his old green truck.

Cat favored Annie Bowen with a rare, cool smile. "Yeah, I gotta admit, the room's not bad," she purred. "For a change, maybe old lady Allen knew what she was doing."

After eleven o'clock, however, when Cat crawled into her new bed on the darkened front porch, she wasn't sure that was true.

The problem was, on the first night in a place she'd never slept in before, Cat always got a peculiar, anxious feeling. She didn't like to admit it, but she felt the same way she had the time she was coming home from first grade, had turned the corner too soon, and all of a sudden discovered that she was lost.

During the day, see, no matter what a person was doing, it

28

was pretty easy not to feel lost or lonely, but at night when you were finally in bed and all the lights were out, it wasn't so simple. For one thing, each new place had its own sounds. Take this queer little pink house, for instance. Tonight it was creaking and sighing to itself as if it were telling itself a bedtime story that only it knew the ending of.

It didn't help much, either, when Cat noticed some strange, sparkling gizmos above the edges of the black trees that surrounded the yard beyond the windowpanes. Fireflies? she wondered uneasily. Did they bite or sting? She sat up in bed and strained to see better.

Oh! Stars. Somehow they seemed a lot brighter and closer out here in the boonies than they ever had in the park. On Harley Street, of course, you never noticed stars at all; the neon glitz and glitter ate up the night and made anything as ordinary as a star totally invisible.

Then Cat stiffened. She pulled the quilt up and held it tight against her chest. The door across the room was opening slowly. She was pretty sure she'd closed it, though. Cat waited, poised, her pulse thundering in her ears, ready to fly out of bed and toward one of the porch windows. A second later she heard a soft snick-snick on the bare wood floor, and a pale blur, indistinct as a phantom, moved across the room toward her.

The scroungy yellow dog, which once had been a puppy as pretty as a bowl of peaches and cream, limped solemnly to the edge of the bed, the sound of his last few steps muffled as he crossed the braided rug. Cat bent toward him while he peered up at her with cloudy eyes. In the faint star shine that filled the room, she could see that his muzzle was frosted with silver hairs. For a long moment the dog studied her pensively, somewhat as a nearsighted grandfather might have.

"Hey, pooch, do you want to get up here?" Cat inquired.

At the sound of her voice, however, the old dog turned away and hobbled back to his own bed, a basket that Cat had noticed earlier under the table in Annie's kitchen. To her amazement, she felt a twinge of disappointment. She'd hoped the old mutt might decide to jump up on the bed and keep her company through the night. But to him *I'm still a stranger*, she realized; *as far as he's concerned, I don't belong here yet, and by the time he gets used to me, I'll be ready to hit the road again.*

It wasn't cold, but when Cat lay down again, she tugged the quilt up to her chin. At its edge she traced the outline of its neatly sewn patches with her fingertips. One summer—oh, she must've been about seven years old—Gram had made a quilt just like this one, a patchwork of soft dream colors, the corner of each patch tacked down with a piece of bright yard tied in a square knot. She hadn't thought about Gram for a long time, Cat realized. When she'd left home a year ago, had she decided to forget everything, Gram included?

But apartment 272A at the project had never been home, not like Gram's house when they all still lived there. At 272A, Mom kept the drapes drawn against the intrusion of fresh air and sunshine; the sink was always full of dirty dishes; the table was usually covered with stale food and ashtrays that overflowed. Home hadn't really been home for a long time.

Sometimes, five or six days went by when Mom never got dressed at all. She was a permanent lump on the couch, her old red bathrobe snugged around herself, enveloped in a blue haze of cigarette smoke. She spent her afternoons absorbed in *All My Children* and *As the World*

Turns. She didn't begin to show signs of life until about five o'clock when Danny or Joe or Larry (their names changed so often that Cat didn't try to keep track of who was who anymore) came around with a sackful of burgers and a six-pack of beer.

Slowly, the old gardener's bungalow ceased its storytelling. The room on the slant-floored porch became so quiet that the only thing Cat heard was the sound of her own heartbeat. Well, I might as well stay here a couple of days, she decided, especially now that I know about Hooter Lewis and his green truck. When morning comes, she comforted herself, I'll figure out what my long-range plans are. In the bright light of day, it was always easier to decide where to go, what to do next.

4

At eight o'clock the next morning Cat found herself hunched over the tiny table in the beekeeper's crowded kitchen. Her bare feet bumped into Peaches's bed underneath; she rested her heels on the floor and curled her toes over the edge of his basket.

The plate in front of Cat had been loaded with sausage, and two fried eggs stared up at her like a pair of astonished yellow eyes. In the middle of the table was a stack of enough buttered toast to feed a family of four. The sight and smell of so much food so early in the morning had always been a stomach-turner for Cat. Her personal preference regarding the proper way to start a day was with a cigarette, an ice-cold Pepsi, and a candy bar—in that order—and none of them before noon at the earliest.

"Uh, listen, I'm not exactly a breakfast person." Cat groaned, shoving her plate far enough away that the two yellow eyes couldn't ogle her reproachfully. "It's not my thing, see; food this early makes me feel kinda yucky." If Annie felt insulted, that was her problem.

"Hey, my fault!" Annie exclaimed cheerfully. Cat gritted her teeth; too much goodwill the first thing in the morning also grated on her nerves.

"I guess I forget that not everybody has an appetite like mine," Annie confessed, and clapped a large hand on one of her own well-padded hips to indicate that she knew she was a big eater and that every bite showed. "So how about a piece of dry toast and a glass of orange juice instead?" she asked, and without waiting for an answer, stuck a piece of bread into the toaster. "My mama used to say that dry toast was good medicine for a morning tummy."

People who said tummy instead of belly and mama instead of mom bugged Cat. She scowled and nibbled on the piece of warm, unbuttered toast that Annie handed to her. The orange juice, in a pretty glass with white daisies on it, tasted as if it had been freshly squeezed. Special for me, Cat wondered, to make a good first impression?

She hated to deal with all that again, with one more foster mother who was determined to make a difference, and kept a noncommittal look pasted on her face as the beekeeper turned the unwanted eggs and sausage into the dog's dish near the back door. A moment later, Cat felt Peaches brush against her bare feet as he struggled out of his bed under the table. He didn't gobble the food wolfishly, as a younger dog might have, but seemed to savor each small bite.

"Well, I suppose you've been asking yourself what in

the world a person does on a bee farm," Annie suggested after she plopped herself down and attacked her own breakfast.

"Not really," Cat murmured drily. This lady still takes it for granted that we're going to end up on friendly terms, she realized. All the hints she'd dropped yesterday hadn't registered yet with Annie, Cat brooded, but then who could read the mind of a foster mother? Most of them believed that all that was needed to turn someone else's life around was a little TLC, a clean bed, some good food. Worse, they figured you believed it too.

Nothing could be further from the truth, Cat knew she'd have to inform Annie Bowen. The only reason I'm sitting across this table from you, she'd explain, is because some skinny, blue-haired social worker hauled me out here and dumped me off. I'm not here of my own free will, got it? As for wondering what a person did on a bee farm—who cared?

"Being a bee farmer wasn't anything I ever intended to be," Annie told her, "if you'll excuse the pun." She seemed oblivious to the bored look Cat shot in her direction.

"Before my friends suggested raising bees, I tried to raise chickens and sell eggs," Annie confessed. "Trouble was, I couldn't really compete with the big, fancy commercial egg producers in the area, so I gave up on that. Those three chickens you saw out in the yard are the remains of my great egg-laying empire."

When Annie smiled ruefully, remembering the downfall of what was to have been her means of livelihood, Cat noticed that her hazel-colored eyes smiled too. "That was almost eighteen years ago, and now I'm a fixture in these parts." Annie chortled. "'Annie Bowen, the Bee Lady'—well, I guess I could've done a lot worse with my life."

"I sure don't see how," Cat considered retorting. Who'd call a crummy pink house, an old yellow dog, and a bunch of bees a good life? The whole conversation had convinced Cat of one thing: the time had come to turn off the beekeeper. Permanently. This intimate, let's-be-friends business had gone too far.

Cat set her half-finished glass of orange juice on the checkered tablecloth and shoved her plate of toast away. The moment had arrived to put a little curl in old Annie Bowen's hair.

"How much did Mrs. Allen tell you about me?" Cat began, a sly smile tugging at the corners of her mouth.

The question seemed to take Annie by surprise. "Oh, not much," she answered with a shrug. "Let's see—she said you'd left home. Had dropped out of school. That a couple of other foster homes hadn't worked out. This was to be your third and last placement, she said. Basic stuff, you know. Mrs. Allen seemed to believe that a place like this—" The beekeeper waved a large brown hand to include the kitchen, Peaches drowsing near the back door, the view beyond the window. "—that a place like Sweetberry might be exactly what you needed." She smiled, showing her large, horsey teeth. "That's about all, I guess."

Cat lowered her glance, leaned her elbows on the table, and studied the red checks on the tablecloth. This was going to be a zinger; she savored such moments, when she got the chance to shock the socks off someone like Annie or Mrs. Allen.

35

"Those welfare people have a name for girls like me," she murmured silkily. Boy, the Wilsons and Turners sure had a hard time swallowing the bad news when she'd laid it on them.

"Promiscuous, that's what they call me," she purred. "Pro-miss-kew-us," she repeated, caressing each syllable, just in case Annie hadn't gotten the message. "You know what that means, bee lady?"

It was Annie's turn to rest her elbows on the table. "Sure, Cat, I know what it means," she replied evenly, leaning forward as she spoke. Her eyes no longer smiled, but she didn't look especially mad or scared either. "And my name's Annie, in case it slipped your mind," she added matter-of-factly. Her cheeks hadn't turned pink, the way Mrs. Wilson's had, Cat observed with disappointment. Okay, maybe what the old gal needed was a more graphic description.

"It means I like to get it on with guys," Cat murmured, pleased by the cool, threatening tone in her voice. "See, people like you and Mrs. Allen have got all these stupid rules and ideas that don't fit people like me. You've got these lists of shoulds and shouldn'ts and do's and don'ts, which is all you know about. You don't know how it feels when a guy—"

"You don't need to draw me a picture," Annie countered mildly. Her voice hadn't raised an octave, and she wasn't chewing on her lip the way Mrs. Allen did. "But it seems to me that if you'd really enjoyed what you were doing, Cat, you wouldn't sound so mad about it now," the beekeeper observed in a pensive way that enraged Cat.

Mad? Listen, Annie Bowen had to be crazy to believe

such a thing! It didn't help, either, to realize it was Annie who was supposed to have gotten rattled and disconcerted by this conversation. "Hey, you old bag, what I did was *fun!*" Cat insisted hotly. "Nobody ever made me do anything I didn't want to do real bad myself, got that? And I bet the next time I decide to get naked with some dude, it'll be—"

Before she could launch into a colorful account of what the next time would be like, a crunch of tires sounded on the gravel in the driveway outside. Through the window next to the kitchen table Cat could see that an old green truck had come to a stop near the back door.

"It's Hooter," Annie announced, pleased. "The mail must've come in early this morning; usually he doesn't come by until about eleven." Cat waited for the beekeeper to issue a frantic order not to dare mess around with Hooter Lewis, who was sweet and seventeen, but Annie merely turned to watch Peaches jump up, his feather-duster yellow tail making his whole rear end wag in an eager greeting.

Hooter Lewis walked into the kitchen without bothering to knock. Like he owns the joint, Cat thought peevishly, and felt inclined to dislike him even before she got to know him.

"So how's it going, Anna Banana?" He hailed the beekeeper breezily and laid a wooden package about fourteen inches long and eight inches high on the end of the kitchen counter. It was plastered with shipping labels, and he tapped one of them gently with an index finger. "I gave a listen to your new girls before I hauled 'em out here," he confided. "They're talking to each other nice and low, not like that last batch I delivered." Cat saw him

37

flick a glance in her direction and was miffed that he didn't seem surprised to see her sitting in Annie's kitchen.

"The last batch of bees that Hooter's talking about had to be replaced," Annie explained. "There was a layer of dead bees on the bottom of the shipping cage that was two bees deep and getting deeper as we watched. Dealers are always real good about replacing a batch that hasn't traveled well, so it didn't actually mean any money out of my pocket, thank heavens."

"You need some help getting these new gals settled?" Hooter wanted to know, and plunked himself down at the breakfast table without waiting to be invited. He helped himself to the last piece of buttered toast, smothered it with honey, and eyed the coffeepot expectantly. Annie poured a cup for him and shoved it across the table.

"Not this time, Hoot. Cat, here, will give me a hand if I need it." The beekeeper smiled. "By the way, meet Cat Kincaid. She already knows who you are; we saw you pass by yesterday, and I apprised her of all your sterling qualities."

Hooter accepted the praise without a blink, wiped his palm on the leg of his jeans, and stuck his hand across the table. "Howdy, Cat," he mumbled around a mouthful of toast. "Pleased to meetcha. Neat name," he observed.

"That's because I'm a real neat kid," Cat purred huskily. She narrowed her green eyes, knowing from hours of practice in a mirror just how emeraldlike and promising she could make them look. She gave Hooter a slow, lazy smile. The Look—that's how she thought of it. The Look had worked its magic on every guy she'd ever used it on. It was calculated to be partly soft and partly tough, partly innocent and partly wild. The Look made no demands, but it promised volumes. Cat leaned back in her chair, the better to treat Hooter to a clear view of the red rose on her T-shirt and the shapely flesh that it covered.

Hooter Lewis, unfortunately, didn't pick up on the message she intended to deliver.

"Listen, my eyes used to bother me a lot too around this time of year," he said sympathetically. "It's all the pollen around these parts; that stuff might be okay for Annie's bees, but it's the pits for people like you and me who've got allergies."

Cat blinked in disbelief. The guy was a dork! "I don't have allergies!" she hissed indignantly. At first, he'd seemed kind of cute; his hair was dark and thick, and the eyes behind the tinted aviator glasses were the color of ripe olives. Too bad that she'd have to revise her opinion, but if he was too dense to pick up on the Look, it'd sure be too much effort to make him want to take a trip to Florida with her. Yesterday, she'd thought it might be interesting to hustle him; today, the benefits of doing so seemed exceedingly chancey.

"You're going to like it here," Hooter went on, oblivious to the golden opportunity he'd just let pass by. His brown eyes held her green ones with a steady, matter-of-fact glance. "I've met all of Annie's girls, and if they were right here now, they'd tell you what a great old gal she is." He gave Cat a wink and jerked a thumb in Annie's direction.

"Waaaaaait a minute," Annie objected loudly. "I might be old enough to be your mother, but your grandmother I'm not!"

Hooter gulped his coffee, jumped up from the table,

wrapped Annie in a bear hug, and planted a kiss on her cheek. Watching them with narrowed eyes, Cat thought: My, my, what a cozy pair! She was a little surprised at how left out their antics made her feel; it was worse when Annie kissed Hooter right back. They were as revolting as the Turners had been, Cat consoled herself, who were always delivering pats and hugs and squeezes to each other. Stuff like that was crap; it was the way people acted when they knew someone else was watching, as if they were auditioning for a commercial on TV. Cat yawned enormously and turned, bored again, to stare through the kitchen window.

"Gotta hit the road now," she heard Hooter declare. "See ya, Anna Banana," he called cheerily and, when he got to the door, added over his shoulder, "and you too, Cat. Maybe we can get together sometime, huh?" He doesn't know that as far as I'm concerned, he just died, Cat realized. "I'll call you, okay?" he suggested. Cat didn't bother to answer, but since he bounded out the door without waiting for one, the snub went unnoticed. By the time you get around to calling, buddy, I'll be back on Harley Street, she promised herself grimly.

As the sound of Hooter's tires on the gravel died away, Annie began to stack the breakfast dishes. "I'll let these soak while I mix up some syrup for the new bees," she announced, and, since there wasn't anything else to do, Cat watched the beekeeper measure two cups of water into a small pan and set it to boil. When the water began to bubble, she added two cups of white sugar and kept stirring until it was dissolved. Next she set the pan in a larger one filled with ice cubes and let the mixture cool.

Cat scooted her chair back from the table when Annie moved the wooden box from the countertop to the kitchen table, got a pastry brush from a drawer, and settled herself in front of the container, which, Cat saw, had a small screened window in each of its two largest sides.

"Want to take a peek before I feed them?" Annie invited.

Cat made an ugly face and shook her head. "I told you I wasn't into bees," she growled. She hoped that Annie didn't intend to take the cover off the box; the whole house would be full of bees, and it'd be impossible to coax them all back into it again.

"These ladies have been traveling for three days," Annie remarked, eyeing the dates on the shipping labels, "which means they're probably pretty hungry by now. It's a good idea to give new bees a good meal before taking them into the field; well-fed bees are sure easier to handle than hungry ones, believe me."

Annie poured a cup of the cooled syrup into a bowl, dipped the pastry brush into it, and began to drizzle the liquid onto the screened sides of the box. Within moments, Cat heard the humming sound that came from within grow louder and more energetic.

"You're really making a mess on the tablecloth," Cat pointed out sourly. "That stuff's running right out the other side of that box, in case you hadn't noticed."

"I should've spread a newspaper on the table before I started," Annie admitted. "What I want to do, you see, is make sure the bees have a nice puddle of syrup inside the cage to feed from." She finished drizzling the bowl of syrup into the cage then set the box on the piece of newspaper she'd neglected to use during the first phase of her operation.

41

"Do me a favor, will you, Cat?" Annie asked. "Fold up this tablecloth and set it over there on the washing machine, okay? I'll run it through later this afternoon." She picked up the cage, held the newspaper under it to catch last-minute drips, and headed for the basement stairs. "It's cool and dark down here, and the bees will rest nicely until we take them out to the field." She paused at the door leading to the basement.

"It's kind of neat, come to think of it!" she exclaimed suddenly.

"What is?" Cat groaned, wishing only that night would come so she could start off down the road and get back to Harley Street.

"That you and my new bees got here at almost the same time." The beekeeper smiled. Cat steadfastly resisted returning the smile. "Maybe it's a good omen, huh?" Annie pressed.

"I'm not into omens any more'n I'm into bees," Cat replied, but Annie was already halfway down the stairs and probably didn't hear the bad news. Cat studied the puddle of sugar syrup, a dark stain in the middle of the tablecloth. Should she clean it up, as Annie had asked? Cat sat motionlessly in her chair. Naw, she decided; to cooperate might only convince Annie Bowen there was hope that this third placement would work out.

But it wasn't going to, Cat realized without regret. Tonight, as soon as the old ditz was asleep, she'd be out one of those windows on the porch and would head up the road as soundlessly as a jungle cat. She'd slip from shadow to shadow along that aisle lined by pines and poplars, her way lighted only by the star shine that last night had filled her bedroom. As soon as she got to the highway, she'd begin to hitch her way north.

42

Should she leave Annie a note? Cat wondered. Forget it; too corny. She'd just leave, period, as she'd left the Wilsons and Turners. All that really mattered was getting back to Harley Street, to Davey's apartment above the Used Goods Galore store, to all the people who hung out at the Hideout. Annie Bowen was welcome to keep her Mr. Sun, her senile yellow dog, her dumb bees—Cat Kincaid intended to go back to real life.

5

At four o'clock, as the shadows began to lengthen in the unmowed grass around the gardener's bungalow, Annie went outside to back an old Jeep out of its stall in a dilapidated shed next to the house. Cat watched critically from the kitchen window as Annie turned the vehicle around and pointed its nose toward the road. She hoped she wouldn't be asked to go wherever it was that Annie was headed.

No such luck, she realized crankily when Annie clomped into the house a moment later. "I've already given the bees a second feeding," the beekeeper announced cheerily, "so as soon as we get our clothes changed, we can take right off."

Cat frowned darkly at the news, disgruntled that all of her irritable frowns and scowls since arriving at Sweetberry had so far gone mostly unnoticed by Annie Bowen. And what was this crap about changing clothes? Cat glanced down approvingly at her black jeans, black shirt, black granny boots.

"So what's wrong with what I've got on?" she demanded. Black was tough; how could a person keep on being a leopard woman if she didn't wear black and keep herself hard and dangerous?

"Bees don't care much for dark colors," Annie explained. "As far as a bee is concerned, anything large and dark spells bad news."

"Give me a break," Cat countered, convinced that Annie's real problem was that she personally didn't like tight black jeans and snug black T-shirts. "I'll bet bees don't know good news from bad news," she added sarcastically.

Annie only shrugged and smiled. "Bees have been domesticated for thousands of years, of course, but someone told me once that they've inherited their ancestors' memories of having had their hives raided by bears. Apparently dark hulks still spell b-e-a-r to them."

Cat glowered and watched Annie pluck a white cotton jumpsuit off a hook inside the closet door. A second suit hung next to it. Eloise, Liza, and Betsy had probably heard this story too, she speculated sourly. "If you change your mind, you can hop into that other suit," Annie murmured amiably. "There's an extra hat and bee veil on the top shelf, and a pair of white tennies about your size on the floor of the closet."

"Hat and veil?" Cat snorted. "You planning to marry me off or what?"

Annie laughed. "Not exactly. Bring them along, though. You'll find out why when we get to the field." The beekeeper proceeded to suit up by pulling the white jumpsuit on over her jeans and shirt, then changing into

45

white socks and white high-topped tennies with Velcro fasteners.

Cat snatched the second bee suit off its hook, fiddled with its zipper, and debated about putting it on. Face it, she told herself. The prospect of being mistaken for a bear and having to fight off hundreds of angry bees was not exactly a thrill. With a groan she pulled the suit on over her black outfit. As she struggled to put on the socks and tennies, though, she started to perspire like crazy. She fanned her armpits and groaned loudly.

Annie nodded. "Yeah, I gotta admit that's the not-so-great part about bee suits—they're as hot as portable saunas," she admitted, and wiped the back of her brown hand across her own shiny forehead.

It was a relief to get into the Jeep and, five minutes later, to have the air rush past as they flew down the highway. Annie, the wind tearing at her chopped-off hair, proceeded to tell Cat more stuff about bees than she cared to know.

"As I mentioned yesterday, my bees are an Italian strain, which of course aren't the only kind of bees a person can keep. A friend of mine has Caucasians, and he swears they're easier to handle. A gal over in Dodge County keeps Carniolans, but she admits they tend to swarm too easily."

Annie leaned toward Cat as if the subject was of deep mutual interest. "I guess what I like best about Italians is that they're workaholics, like me. In a good year, I can count on 'em producing more'n three hundred pounds of honey per hive," she beamed. Cat steadfastly continued to frown. Annie nattered on about how pretty her bees were—a soft, golden color, she said—but Cat, bored, tuned her out and wondered, instead, who might be at the Hideout right now.

At this very moment, as she was flying down this dumb highway out here in the boonies (where she'd been taken against her will, never having asked anyone for help), Cat mused, were the guys who'd gathered at the Hideout to chugalug a few beers and smoke a few joints wondering where *she* was?

Cat imagined that someone back there was asking: "Hey, what ever happened to the leopard woman? Anybody seen her lately? That chick ain't been around in a looooong time!" Cat smiled secretly. Yeah, they missed her all right; she'd bet her life on it. And Davey—had he realized yet that she'd borrowed his Bon Jovi tape? She'd know the answer by tomorrow; by this time on Thursday, she'd be right back where she belonged.

The shadows in the fields were tinted a pale blue half an hour later when Annie peeled off the highway onto a road that was even narrower than the one leading to her house. She put the Jeep into four-wheel drive, climbed it up a steep incline, then eased the vehicle down a south-facing slope into a pool of amber sunshine.

Nearby stood several wooden boxes painted white, stacked one on top of the other. The boxes looked just like the one Cat had seen Annie load into the Jeep before they left Sweetberry. The air was filled with a steady hum, but the bees flew back and forth to the hives too swiftly for Cat to tell if they were as golden as Annie claimed they were.

Annie hopped out of the Jeep and reached for her white hat and its attached veil. She clamped the broad-brimmed hat on her head, opened the collar of her bee suit,

47

smoothed the veil against her neck, then zipped the suit shut, creating a secure seal against intruding bees. A bee whizzed past on its way to one of the occupied hives, and Cat hastily did likewise.

"I work bare-handed," Annie remarked, handing Cat a pair of heavy white gloves, "but I don't think you ought to, not until you get used to the bees and they get used to you." That ain't ever gonna happen, Cat considered replying, because by tomorrow this chick will be long gone from this buggy place.

Annie carried the white wooden box from the Jeep to a spot that had recently been cleared of tall grass, removed its metal cover, then returned to the Jeep to collect the package of new bees. She also picked up a peculiar-looking tin can with a lid, handle, and what Cat decided must be a pouring spout.

Cat was startled, then, to see Annie stuff pieces of burlap into the can and drop a match inside. When the material caught fire, she closed the lid and gently pumped a small bellows attached to the side of the can. A moment later, a stream of pale smoke belched from the pouring spout.

"You gonna set fire to your bees?" Cat asked, alarmed. It seemed an awfully cruel fate, even for a bee.

"Nope," Annie answered. "There's something about smoke that pacifies bees and makes them want to feed. With full tummies they can't bend very easily to use their stingers." Deftly, Annie puffed one of the busy nearby hives, and Cat saw for herself that the bees surrounding it immediately rushed inside to eat.

"But if you *do* get stung," Annie warned, "try not to overreact. Translation: don't take a wild swing at the bee and squash it. Number one, quick gestures alarm bees, and number two, the odor released by a dying bee—she'll only sting you once, by the way, and then she dies—smells a little bit like banana oil and is a signal to all her hivemates to come to the rescue."

Cat pulled on the gloves Annie had given to her. Her face behind her own bee veil was greasy with sweat. She knew her eye shadow was probably running into the creases around her eyes; she'd soon look like she'd been drunk for a week. Perspiration ran in rivulets down her sides. Jeez! How could a sane person want to live this way? Cat vowed that even if she stayed at Sweetberry, which, of course, she didn't plan to do, she'd never come out to the fields with Annie again.

Annie cradled the package of new bees under her arm, picked up her smoker, and headed up the slope toward the new hive. "Coming?" she called over her shoulder.

Cat braced her rear end against the fender of the Jeep. Her body odor, pungent and sweaty, rose through the collar of her bee suit, reminding her how miserable and out of place she felt. She ought to have trusted her intuition, refused to come out here with Annie in the first place. Cat groaned softly to herself. The only thing that mattered now was for this stupid day to end, for night to fall so she could take off. Night, however, was still several hours away, so with another persecuted groan, Cat trudged up the slope behind the beekeeper.

Annie hefted the box of bees under her arm. "This weighs about three pounds," she informed Cat, "which is equivalent to three thousand bees. They're well fed, though, and with evening coming on we won't have any trouble getting them settled." *We*, Cat noticed; Annie still hadn't wised up to the fact it would never be we.

The beekeeper pried up a small wooden cover on the

package of bees and removed a much smaller container. "Did I mention that I ordered a new queen this time?" she asked. "Yep—she's a Starmaker, one of the finest Italian hybrids available. Look, she even travels in her own private compartment," Annie explained, and beckoned Cat to come closer. "Here she is, with a dozen attendants."

"What's she need attendants for?" Cat wheezed, short of breath and wishing she could reach under her veil to wipe the salty perspiration out of her eyes.

"A queen bee has become so specialized that she can't feed or groom herself," Annie explained. "She only leaves the hive once, on her mating flight, during which she is fertilized and then never mates again."

Wow, some sex life, Cat reflected; you did it once, then never again. No wonder Annie felt a kinship with bees.

Annie peered into the queen cage. "Here, take a look," she invited again.

Cat, sweat clouding her vision, could barely distinguish a darkish lump in one corner of the cage. Looking at the outside of the box, however, she noted that a round hole in one end of it had been plugged with a piece of cork, while a hole in the opposite end was sealed with what appeared to be a piece of hard white candy.

"That's what it is, all right," Annie told her. "Candy— that's what the queen and her entourage have been feeding on since they left the supplier three days ago."

Annie set the queen's cage aside and held the larger bee package over the open hive. Cat expected bees to fly out and head off in every direction, but instead, a mass of bees, clinging to each other to form a ball, dropped into the hive. When a few bees stubbornly resisted making the transfer, Annie took a small brush from a pocket in her bee suit and gently swept them out into their new home.

"Listen to that sweet, low hum," Annie directed. "That's a good sound—curious, but contented. If you hear a high-pitched *beeeooo,* though, beware! It's the sound that probably earned them their name; our word bee comes from the Anglo-Saxon *beo,* inspired, I'll wager, from the noise that angry bees make."

Next, Annie tacked the small queen cage between two vertical hive frames in the center of the hive, its candy plug facing downward. "It'll take the bees a couple of days to chew through that plug," she explained, "and by that time the workers will be acquainted with the queen's pheromones, or odors. If I dumped her straight in with the others, the workers might accidentally smother her, leaving us with no new queen."

Us, Cat heard. Well, Annie apparently was doomed to feel pretty bad, all right, when she discovered that the bed on the front porch hadn't been slept in tonight, that no way was there ever going to be an us. Cat sighed and felt a flicker of pity for the beekeeper who, for some reason, seemed compelled to assume so much that could never be true.

By the time Annie had checked her other hives, the shadows on the hillside were deep blue and the air had begun to cool. She jumped happily behind the wheel of her Jeep, and Cat, sweaty and grouchy, climbed in on the passenger's side.

"Getting a new queen settled always calls for a celebration," the beekeeper declared, stripping her hat and veil from her head. "Let's go home, take turns in the shower, and I'll throw a couple of steaks on the grill. How's that sound?"

"Whatever," Cat answered, careful not to show any enthusiasm that might be misinterpreted. Steaks sounded good, but there was no sense in making Annie think they had a future together. Cat took off her own hat and hoped she'd be able to get into the shower first; she couldn't remember a time when she'd stunk so bad. Annie, however, was in high spirits, and as they flew down the highway on their way back to Sweetberry, she insisted on pointing out all the different sorts of plants and flowers the bees liked to feed on.

"White clover is truly their favorite," she chattered, "which is handy since it blooms all year long and can be found almost everywhere." Cat heard that dandelions provided lots of pollen but made a bitter-tasting honey, that wild mustard and goldenrod were important foods, that pollen and nectar from all the gardens in the township were also gathered by the bees.

Cat tried to close her ears to Annie's ramblings; didn't the old bat ever run out of steam? she wondered. When Annie turned the Jeep near the yellow vine-covered sign advertising Home of the Sweetest Taste This Side of Paradise, Cat saw something that annoyed her even more. A green truck flew past, and a lean brown arm waved a greeting from the driver's side. She caught a fleeting glimpse of dark eyes behind a pair of aviator glasses and could plainly see that Hooter Lewis was not alone. His passenger was a girl with short, curly yellow hair, who, in Cat's opinion, sat closer to him than she really needed to.

"I'm gonna call you!" Hooter cried. "I haven't forgotten!"

The truck was swallowed up in dust, and Cat glowered. "So who's the chick?" she wondered out loud to Annie.

"The chick? If you mean that blond girl, that's Shirl."

Shirl, the squirrel. "So he's got a girlfriend, right?"

"Hooter's got lots of friends who are girls, but I'm not sure he's got a girlfriend." Annie laughed. "Shirl's mom and dad run the drugstore over in Channing. I think Shirl works there in the summer."

Cat felt a familiar, gnawing hunger take hold of her. It was the same feeling she'd often had when she walked the hallways at Jefferson before she wised up and dropped out of the stupid place.

The thing was, everybody had somebody. Anyplace you went in school, it was the same. People walked down the halls or into rooms in pairs or bunches. Even the nerdy types hung out with other nerdy types. Everyone belonged. In the beginning, Cat remembered, when she'd been new at Jefferson, she'd tried so hard to fit in, to make a place for herself, but nothing had ever worked, and at the end she was as much an outsider as she'd been on the first day.

When she'd found the Used Goods Galore store, it'd been by accident. She'd only gone there to buy some funky clothes, thinking that if she couldn't belong at Jefferson, she'd make darn sure she looked like she didn't, and had ended up meeting Floss and Angie. Afterward, fitting in at school mattered less and less.

The decision to leave the project, come to think of it, had been an accident too. It was a process of just drifting away, sleeping a night or two at Floss's or Angie's, until finally a decision was reached before she'd actually made up her mind. Staying away just turned out to be easier, Cat reflected, than going back to the project and discovering that Mom had another new "friend."

Cat caressed her white-clad knees. But what exactly did all that have to do with seeing Hooter and Shirl together a minute ago? Cat asked herself. She felt jealous and wanted to get even with them, but hey, she didn't even know them yet, so what was the big problem? Did it have anything to do with that crap Mrs. Allen peddled, Cat wondered uneasily, that stuff about acting out? The suspicion that it might made her feel edgy.

Annie wheeled the Jeep expertly into its shed beside the pink bungalow. "Tell you what, Cat. Why don't you hop into the shower first?" she suggested. "While you're doing that, I'll get some charcoal started in the grill, and when I'm cleaning up, you can make a salad. Okay?"

Cat nodded but resolutely didn't make a salad while Annie took her turn in the shower. Annie fixed it herself as she grilled the steaks, and Cat was a little disappointed that the beekeeper didn't get on her case about it. Instead, Annie squinted shrewdly at her across the supper table and mumbled around a mouthful of steak, "You know what I think is the most unusual thing about bees?"

No, Cat thought, irritation making her jaw muscles tighten, but I'll bet a million bucks you're gonna tell me. She stabbed at a piece of steak on her own plate and avoided the beekeeper's level glance.

"The destiny of bees is programmed into their genetic code. A queen is a queen, a worker is a worker, a drone is a drone. They never have to decide what they'll do next or how they're going to live their lives." Annie helped herself to some salad, and from under lowered lashes Cat saw the beekeeper pause with a wedge of tomato halfway to her mouth.

"Being human is so much harder," Annie went on. Cat studied her own plate and refused to appear interested.

"We're free," Annie murmured, "and that's never an easy thing to be—if you'll excuse the feeble pun."

"Feeble isn't the word for it," Cat growled. She felt Peaches stir under the table and snaked a piece of meat down to him. "And if it's all the same to you, I don't need any more lectures, okay?"

As soon as Annie was in bed, Cat put her escape plan into operation. First, she'd turn off her own bedside light but would merely rest on top of the quilt until Annie was asleep, then would slip soundlessly through one of the porch windows and be gone for good. Her light hadn't been out five minutes, however, before she heard a familiar snick-snick on the bare wood floor and glanced across the room to see a pale blur move slowly toward her.

She rolled onto her stomach and peered down. Peaches looked up with patient, milky brown eyes.

"So what're you trying to tell me, muttzo?" Cat asked gruffly. When the dog didn't turn around at the sound of her voice, she quizzed him again. "You trying to tell me you want to get up here with me tonight? It won't do you any good, y'know, since I don't plan to stick around for more'n about ten minutes," she informed him. The old yellow dog continued to study her solemnly, so Cat relented at last and patted the edge of the bed.

"Okay, okay, so hop up here already." She waited for him to leap eagerly onto the bed, and when he didn't, it dawned on Cat that it was because he couldn't. With a grunt she crawled off the bed and tried to hoist him up. The old dog was a lot heavier than she expected, so she propped his front paws on the edge of the bed, then boosted his back end up.

Peaches stood spraddle-legged in the middle of the bed, surprised to find himself there, and Cat lay down herself. After pondering his situation a moment, the dog lowered himself fanny-first onto the quilt, then let his front legs slide out from under him. He rested his nose on his forepaws and blinked at Cat.

"Now what's your problem?" she demanded. She felt his tail thump once against her leg. She rolled onto her side and put an arm around his lumpy shoulder. His fur was silky, but he had an unmistakably doggy odor. It was a cozy smell, though, so Cat took a deep whiff of it. She'd never had a dog; pets weren't allowed at the project, of course. Once, when she'd been about nine or ten and they'd still lived with Gram, they'd had a white cat named Sissy, but it had to be given away when they moved.

Peaches began to snore softly in Cat's ear. Beyond the window, she could see the stars pulse in the inky sky. In another few minutes she'd be out there, under that sky. It came as a surprise, however, to discover that with her arm around Peaches's shoulder she didn't really feel like taking off. What she felt like, Cat reflected, was simply a girl who was sleeping on a slant-floored porch with a dog. Period.

Jeez! Cat swallowed a yawn. It was getting hard to stay awake, so she concentrated on Hooter Lewis. "I'm gonna call you!" he'd promised. "I haven't forgotten!" he'd cried.

Well, what was the harm in staying at Sweetberry for a couple days longer, just to see if he really meant it? Cat yawned a second time. Look, until then, she'd pretend she was someone who'd come to spend a few weeks with her aunt, who happened to live on a farm where she raised bees. She'd make believe she'd done it every summer since she was a little kid, that her aunt had never been married and didn't have kids of her own.

Cat felt herself sink into a soft lake of sleep and locked her fingers securely in Peaches's silky, odiferous coat. One more night didn't mean she'd decided to stay forever, she reminded herself. When morning came, she could always change her mind again.

6

A whole week passed without a call from Hooter Lewis.

Cat couldn't decide what surprised her most: that he hadn't bothered to call or that she'd hung around like a dope, waiting. It definitely was not her style to wait for anybody, Cat reflected, but excused her indecision on the grounds that Annie had kept her so busy that seven days had passed almost too quickly to be counted.

On Tuesday, however, when Hooter flew past the pink bungalow with yet another call-you-soon-I-haven't-forgotten cry thrown out the window of his truck, Cat realized that she'd foolishly overstayed her time at Sweetberry. Before she left, though, there was one thing she'd promised herself to do.

"Hey, d'you mind if I go over there and take a look at that old house of horrors?" she asked Annie, and jerked a thumb in the direction of the mansion that stood, haunted and blind, in the weed-choked yard two blocks away.

Annie, crouched over her tomato plants, was dusting

each one with a greenish powder. Her strong brown arms glistened with perspiration, and her short gray-brown hair was plastered damply to her round forehead. "No problem." She grunted and looked up with a toothy, good-natured smile.

Am I going to miss that smile? Cat asked herself, startled. Had Annie's easy grin been one of the reasons Eloise, Liza, and Betsy had grown to like the beekeeper so well? No kidding, Annie had turned out to be the best on that list of failed foster mothers. Maybe it had something to do with the fact that Annie was as plain as an old horse, that she'd probably never worried about how she looked to guys, not even when she was young. Cat was certain that nobody'd ever reached for her with a hungry look in his eye and begged her to get naked with him.

The mere idea of Annie and a guy together was sort of comical, and Cat felt a smile tug at the corner of her mouth. After all, who'd want to get it on with a woman who looked more like a farmer than most farmers? Bad off as she was, Cat mused, even Mom tried to trade on what was left of her looks. The only time she showed signs of life was every afternoon when she hauled herself into the bathroom to put on some blusher and eyeliner before one of her "friends" showed up with an inevitable six-pack.

"Would you like some company on your tour?" Annie asked as Cat lingered on the back step. "I'll have these tomatoes finished in about ten minutes. Or would you just as soon wander through the old place all by yourself?"

"I'll go alone," Cat assured her hastily. That was another thing that made Annie so different: she realized a person might like to be alone once in a while. That had been the draggiest part of being a foster kid—whoever took you in felt obliged to be hovering over you every

59

second. Foster parents (the kind she'd gotten, anyway) figured she'd been neglected, that it was their job to try to make it up to her. What they didn't understand was that some things could never be made up for.

"Just be careful of the stairs over there," Annie warned agreeably as Cat stepped off the back porch. "Last time I checked, I noticed that several of the treads were awfully spongy and rotten."

Cat walked across the weedy yard, looking back over her shoulder once to see if Peaches might come along, but he continued to sleep as soundly in the sun as he had on the first day she'd seen him. She turned to face the mansion again. It was weird, but she'd probably miss that smelly old mutt too. Maybe she'd ask Annie for a snapshot of him; she wouldn't explain why she wanted it but would take it with her tonight when she left Sweetberry.

From two blocks away, the old house looked ruined and decrepit, but the closer Cat got to it, the more she could see that the place wasn't in as bad shape as she'd supposed. Vandals somehow hadn't yet gotten around to busting out the front door, and the afternoon sun that glinted through its panes of beveled glass made the entry to the old house appear nearly as handsome as it must have been in its heyday.

Cat mounted the steps carefully, mindful of Annie's warning, and crossed the wide porch. The doorknob was brass and was embossed with flowers and leaves worn smooth by years of use. Cat turned it; metal parts turned rustily against metal parts, and it took several tries before she was able to let the door swing open.

Inside, the house was empty of furniture. Leaves had blown through the broken windowpanes and lay huddled in all four corners of the living room. Rain-streaked wallpaper hung in faded ribbons from the walls. Cat walked slowly to the middle of the room, only to have her skin prickle with dread when she heard a noise behind her. She whirled; it was only Peaches, who must have waked, noticed she was gone, and followed the scent of her footsteps through the weeds.

Cat knelt and put an arm across the dog's shoulder. "Think anybody like me ever lived here?" she asked him. Peaches listened attentively but didn't seem to know the answer. The question echoed hollowly through the unfurnished house, and Cat realized the question had been a foolish one.

"Any girl who lived here wouldn't have much in common with me," she confessed. The girl who'd lived here would never have run away to a place called the Hideout; she'd never have slept in a different bed every few nights. Her mother wouldn't have been a couch potato; this girl would've had brothers and sisters, a father too, not merely a faded image of a man in a uniform, dead long ago in a war people still argued about.

Cat drifted from room to room, Peaches hobbling at her heel. When she'd finished a tour of the kitchen, dining room, and parlor and found herself back in the living room again, she stopped to rest her hand on the banister of the stairway that curved upward to the second floor. "You better wait for me down here, pooch," she advised the dog. Cat could see that he was relieved to hear he didn't have to go any farther, and so, testing each tread, she ascended to the upper floor.

A wide hallway divided the upper story; the large rooms on either side of it must have been bedrooms, Cat decided. The closets in each were as big as some of the places she'd lived in lately, for instance those three postage-stamp-sized rooms in Davey's apartment on Harley Street. For two hundred bucks a month, though, what could a person expect? Davey's place, with its dirty windows that overlooked an air shaft too gloomy even for pigeons to visit, suddenly seemed thousands of miles and a whole lifetime away.

Stones that had been pitched through the bedroom windows lay in the middle of two of the rooms, and leaves that had blown in filled the still air with a dry, lonesome smell. On a dusty shelf in a closet, Cat found a bird's nest; on the floor were the broken shells of some cream-colored eggs. She looked for a name scratched in the paint on the windowsills; there wasn't one. She searched for a message crayoned on the wallpaper; there wasn't any. To have found a clue about the family who'd once lived in these rooms would have made her feel better.

Cat slumped down on a dusty window seat in the largest bedroom, which overlooked the front yard. She was sure about one thing: if she'd been a daughter in a house like this one, she'd never have become a leopard. Here, she could have gone on being plain old Cathleen Kincaid forever.

Below, an oak tree with wine-colored leaves cast a wide circle of shade on the ground. Cat rested her forehead against the windowpane. The mother in this house had baked cookies, she imagined; when a person got home from school, the whole house would've smelled good, instead of reeking of cigarette smoke and stale beer. At Christmastime, the dining room downstairs no doubt had been filled with grandparents and cousins, their rosy faces smiling in the candlelight.

Cat pulled a knee up to her chest, hugged it with both arms, and rested her chin on her bony kneecap. "In a house like this, I could've always been me," she mused aloud to the empty room. The trouble was, for a long time it hadn't been easy to know exactly who me was. Was me a leopard woman who knew how to take care of herself, or was me someone who needed to be rescued, as the welfare people insisted?

One thing for sure, Cat admitted silently, it was getting harder and harder to be dangerous and predatory all the time. She wondered briefly what it would be like to be ordinary again; she'd quit dyeing her hair, wouldn't shoplift anymore, might even go back to school someday. Cat faced herself in the dusty glass. Today, her eyes weren't especially narrow or calculating; she wore no lip slicker; her hair was pulled back from her face and held with a rubber band. Today, she *was* ordinary, and almost a stranger to herself.

Cat glanced down with a frown. In the yard below, an old green truck had coasted noiselessly into the shade cast by the oak tree. The window on the driver's side was rolled down; a familiar brown arm was hooked over the door. Jeez! A moment later Hooter Lewis climbed out, stretched, scratched his armpit, and stood with arms folded across his belt buckle.

Cat's heart flopped in her chest. "Don't let him look up here and see me!" she prayed aloud to the empty room. She didn't want him to see her with her plain, ordinary face, and besides, now that she'd made up her mind to leave Sweetberry for sure, she didn't want to be tempted to unmake her plans. At that instant, Hooter glanced up. He grinned, crooked a finger, and beckoned her down.

Cat retreated from the window and frantically searched the pockets of her jeans for makeup that she might have stashed there and forgotten. She found a stub of eyeliner pencil, but that was all. While Hooter trotted around to the front door, Cat stroked on eyeliner, using the window as a mirror.

Darn, no eye shadow! Hastily, she wetted a finger with her tongue, smooshed the stub of pencil on her fingertip, then smudged her eyelids with the muddy concoction. Messy, but it was the best she could do. She licked her lips several times to make them shiny, pinched her cheeks to make them glow, loosened her hair from the rubber band, and unbuttoned two extra buttons on her shirt front. She was halfway down the curved staircase when Hooter bounded through into the living room.

"Annie told me this is where you'd be," he boomed. "I suppose you figured I'd never keep my promise, right?"

"Hey, I was so busy I hardly noticed," Cat murmured coolly.

"I'm sorry I didn't get back to you sooner, like I said I would," he apologized. He sounded as if he actually meant it. "I've been working mornings at the P.O., see, then I've had to be down at the 4-H hall practically every night, so I—"

"The 4-H?" Cat echoed. It sounded as if he belonged to a gang, but she was surprised they had such things way out here in the boonies. It sounded as if they even had rigged up a place to meet.

"You never heard of 4-H?" Hooter asked. "Stands for head, heart, hands, health. Kids where you come from, big towns and all, wouldn't know anything about it, I guess." His tone was pitying, and his brown eyes offered condolences.

Cat almost laughed in his face. Head, heart, hands, health—he was kidding, right? Standing close to him, however, she was suddenly warmed by a rush of anticipation.

Upstairs, not five minutes ago, she'd wondered what it might be like to be ordinary again; now, in the hushed intimacy of the deserted old house, filled with its muted light and the mellow smell of dry leaves, Cat knew she wanted only one thing: to be even closer to Hooter Lewis. She longed to see a blaze of desire in those dark eyes; she wanted to be encircled by a pair of eager arms that reached hungrily for her. . . .

"Listen, maybe you'd like to come down some night and watch us practice." Hooter invited, not sounding hungry at all. The eyes behind the aviator glasses were friendly rather than starved. "How about tomorrow?" he suggested suddenly. "I mean, if you and Annie don't have anything special planned. She can come too; what d'you say?"

Cat narrowed her gaze slightly and stared up at Hooter with sleepy green eyes. She circled him, pretending to head for the door, then came lazily around to face him again. "You come to this old place very often?" she asked silkily.

Hooter seemed puzzled by the question. "Here? Naw. Not unless there's something Annie wants me to do here, I mean." His neck was sunburned, Cat noticed, and she studied the pulse that throbbed at the point of his jaw.

"I was just wondering if you, well, you know, ever hung out here with anyone," she purred.

"Hung out here?"

"Yeah. Like with your girlfriend."

"I don't exactly have a girlfriend."

"Not exactly? So what's with the chick I saw you with a week ago?"

"Shirl? I see her a lot because we're both in 4-H. Have been since we were in junior high. We square-dance, see; that's what we've been practicing. In August we're going to do a gig at the Channing County fair."

So he square-danced. She'd been right, then, that he probably didn't know anything about street-smart girls. Cat trailed a fingertip slowly up Hooter's bare arm. He smelled freshly of soap and water; his T-shirt was so white it hurt her eyes. The wish to be ordinary vanished completely from her head. In a few hours she'd be gone from Sweetberry forever, but right now, alone with Hooter in this empty house she could—

Cat leaned forward, parted her lips slightly, and treated Hooter to the Look. She was sure that this time he'd pick up on what it meant. He'd put his arms around her, and for a little while she'd feel so good. It wouldn't be like most of those other times, either, because Hooter himself was different. Afterward, when they'd put their clothes back on, it would still be okay; she wouldn't have that sad, used-up, I've-done-another-dumb-thing feeling. No, because Hooter would hold onto her tight, would tell her that he really liked her, would whisper that she was different from any girl he'd ever known. When she told him she was going to leave Sweetberry forever, he might even beg her to stay.

Instead of reaching for her, however, Hooter took an alarmed step backward. "Annie's sure talked a lot about fixing this old place up," he blurted, his voice cracking in midsentence with more caution than passion.

"My dad told her it'd cost a fortune," he said in a rush. "The foundation's bad, he said; you'd need new footings,

66

he told her. That'd mean floor jacks and pouring fresh cement and all that stuff. Annie went ahead and filled out a form to get a grant from the state, though, so you never know. She just might—"

"Why does the old ditz want to fix up this dump?" Cat murmured huskily. She realized suddenly what Hooter's real problem was: he'd never done it before, and it made him nervous to suspect that he could right now, with her, in the privacy of these deserted, leaf-filled rooms. Hooter took a second step backward, dark eyes alert and wary behind his glasses. Cat followed him with a drowsy smile.

"Annie doesn't like to be called old, remember?" Hooter reminded her. "Anyway, she wasn't fixing it up for herself. She wanted a bigger place for girls like, well, girls like you."

"Girls like me?" Cat whispered, and widened her eyes with feigned astonishment. That meant, then, that he knew he didn't have to be shy.

"I didn't mean that exactly the way it came out." Hooter apologized helplessly. "What I meant was, girls who need help, girls who've had a rough time of it—"

By this time he'd managed to back himself out through the front door and had reached the safety of the porch. Okay, Cat told herself, the other thing that makes him jumpy right now is that it's broad daylight, that somebody might see us. But he'd said he had to practice his square dancing, right? Well, afterward he could meet her here again. Then, in the velvety, warm summer darkness he wouldn't be so uptight. She'd even haul that quilt off Annie's bed on the porch and bring it over here so they'd be comfortable and the floor wouldn't feel so hard.

"Listen," Cat began softly, "why don't you meet me

here tonight when you get through at that hall you talked about?"

"Meet you? Here?"

"Sure. Like around eleven o'clock, okay? There's something I gotta talk to you about."

"There is?" Hooter seemed startled, but there was a rising light in his eyes too. In the dark, Cat was sure, he'd feel a lot braver. When they were together, lying skin to skin, as close as two people could get, he'd finally admit, "Oh, Cat, I never knew it'd be like this—"

"So do you want to meet me or not?" Cat persisted.

"Yeah, sure, I guess so," Hooter agreed, and shifted his weight from one foot to the other. He still wasn't exactly turned on by the prospect of being alone with her, Cat noticed, yet there was an unmistakable eager curiosity in his eyes. "Only can't you tell me now what you want to talk about?" he pleaded.

Cat shook her head solemnly and consulted her watch, the one with the black face that she'd snitched from the desk drawer at the Wilsons. "I better get back to Annie's now," she lied expertly. "I think she said we had to go do something with those stupid bees again."

"So you want me to meet you here after practice? Eleven o'clock, you said?" Hooter mumbled, and leaped sideways off the porch without touching a single stair. Cat nodded, and filled her smile with promise. Hooter nearly tripped over a tree root as he scrambled into the cab of his truck.

"Okay—see you later, then!" he cried, killed the motor once in his eagerness to be gone, and flew down the road like a criminal with a sentence over his head.

Cat hugged herself tightly and imagined the arms around her were Hooter's. Tonight, in the dark, he wouldn't be afraid to hold her as if she were the most important person in the world. Afterward, he'd even admit that he was glad he'd done it, that his first time had been with her. He'd bury his face in the blackness of her hair and would whisper: "You're special, Cat; I knew that the first time I ever saw you."

Peaches limped onto the porch and stood, dim-eyed, watching the dust from the green truck settle back onto the road. Cat crouched beside him and looked into his eyes for reassurance but saw only nearsighted concern.

Listen, she argued silently, none of this was related at all to the crap Mrs. Allen peddled. No way did getting it on with Hooter have anything to do with not facing her real problems. Poor Mrs. Allen's main hang-up was that she only knew how to stick labels on things, to screw up her thin lips and deliver you-know-what'll-happen-if-you-don't-shape-up sermons full of bad news about AIDS and venereal disease and getting pregnant, which, Cat told herself, doesn't have anything to do with me.

What Mrs. Allen didn't know—and certainly never wanted to hear—was how good it felt to be held, to have someone's heart beat against your own, to be told that you mattered, that you were loved.

7

When Cat returned to the bungalow, she discovered that it was not a lie, after all, that Annie had decided to do something with the dumb bees.

"It's been a week since we got that Starmaker queen settled," the beekeeper reminded Cat, "which means we ought to get back to the field and do some checking."

"What's to check?" Cat groaned. Messing around with bees was not part of what she planned to do this afternoon. Instead, she wanted to run some clothes through Annie's washer and take a long shower. Then she'd lotion her whole body until it felt silky, anticipating what Hooter would say when he laid his hands on her bare skin tonight. No way, Cat thought resentfully, did she intend to climb into one of those stupid bee suits again, sweat like a pig, and go off to spy on a bunch of bugs.

"It won't take long," Annie assured her, noting Cat's frown. "It's not a good idea to hassle the bees any more than necessary, so we'll make our trip short and quick."

Okay, okay, Cat decided grudgingly; it probably wouldn't kill her to go with Annie one last time—even though Annie wouldn't guess in a hundred years that it *was* the last time.

"Even if we can't spot the queen, we'll be able to tell right away if the brood cells are being filled with eggs," Annie confided to Cat in her isn't-this-a-great-life manner as they flew down the highway twenty minutes later. "The new workers will hatch in about three weeks; then they'll head for the fields."

"Some life," Cat grumbled sarcastically.

"Maybe that's why it's so short." Annie grinned. Cat flicked a curious glance in the beekeeper's direction. Annie didn't grip her steering wheel with a stranglehold like Mrs. Allen did, and although she'd narrowed her eyes against the sun's glare, she didn't have the squinty, frazzled look that the social worker wore like a permanent mask.

"A worker only lives about six weeks," Annie went on, "so the queen has to lay about two thousand eggs a day to keep her hive at its maximum strength of fifty to sixty thousand gals."

"Gals? Aren't there any guys in a hive?" Cat asked. Jeez! Their lives must be as thrilling as Annie's, right?

"There are only a few drones in each hive," Annie explained, "but the queen and her workers run the whole show—women's lib would love 'em!" Annie laughed and halted the Jeep in a patch of shade. She jumped out of the vehicle, closed up the openings of her bee suit, and deftly stoked up her smoker. "I hope you're paying close attention," she teased, "so in case I break an arm or something, you'll be able to take right over for me."

"Better not count on me for anything like that," Cat

71

advised drily. She refrained from adding, "Not to mention the fact I won't even be here after tonight." Plain, mahogany-skinned old Annie Bowen, who'd never needed to be loved, would be grossed out if she knew what was going to happen at eleven o'clock tonight in that deserted old mansion. Being the sort of woman who needed only bees and an old yellow dog to be happy, Cat thought pityingly, she'd never be able to understand what it was like to lie in the warm circle of a guy's arms and be able to shut out the rest of the world.

Annie lifted out a hive frame and there, on a screen of honeycomb, was what Annie claimed was the Starmaker queen. "Take a look, Cat!" she exclaimed. "I never figured we'd find her so quick, but it's her all right! See how much bigger she is than any of her hivemates and how much paler yellow she is too?"

Reluctantly, Cat peered through the mesh of her bee veil. Sure enough, in the center of the frame was a bee whose body was longer than those of her companions, who seemed to be escorting her across the face of the comb. All of the attending bees faced the queen like spokes of a wheel around its hub, and they rhythmically reached out to stroke her, to offer her food or clean her wings and body. Cat observed that now and then the queen interrupted their attentions and lowered herself into one of the empty six-sided cells in her path.

"What's she doing?" Cat wondered aloud, curious in spite of herself.

"Depositing an egg in each cell. In exactly twenty-one days, a worker will hatch out of that cell, all ready to start her life."

"Which lasts a whole six weeks," Cat reminded the beekeeper tartly. Cat stepped back from the hive, aware that Annie was about to launch into another long, boring discussion about bee habits. Enough was enough, she decided; she checked her watch with a yawn and made sure Annie saw her do so.

"You need to get home for something?" the beekeeper asked.

Sweetberry wasn't home, Cat wanted to explain, and it would never be, no more than the project had ever been. "I guess I'm a little pooped today." Cat fibbed easily in a voice that she deliberately made weary and exhausted. "I think I'll hit the sack early tonight. Maybe I'll feel better tomorrow." She'd feel better, all right, because she'd be back on Harley Street.

Annie lowered the frame back in its place and covered the hive. "Sounds good to me too," she declared eagerly. "I've got to get up early and go into Channing tomorrow. Maybe you'd like to ride in with me." Annie loosened the collar of her bee suit and took off her hat and veil. "I have to stop at the drugstore too. If you come with me, you could meet Shirl."

"Swell." Cat lied again. She needed to meet Shirl about as much as she needed a case of herpes, right? Tomorrow morning, of course, she'd be sleeping soundly until noon in one of the none-too-clean beds in Davey Gibson's stuffy but familiar apartment, would get up to her favorite breakfast of a cigarette, a Pepsi, a candy bar.

Once she was back in town, though, she'd have to lie low. As soon as Annie squealed that she was missing, those welfare freaks would be hot on her trail for sure. She'd stick close to Davey's place, wouldn't show her face on Harley Street, would stay away from the Hideout too. Oh, sure, they'd catch up with her eventually, but with a little luck she'd be able to outfox them until summer was over. Cat smiled privately, relishing what it would feel like to be back where she belonged.

"Hey, that's nice," Annie commented, pleased. "I'm so glad to see you smile, Cat! I know that it's never easy to settle into a new place—especially a place that's as unusual as a bee farm—but I hope it's getting easier every day for you to be at Sweetberry with Peaches and me." The beekeeper's gray-brown eyes were warm and gentle and, well, sort of sweet.

Cat hastily averted her own gaze and scrubbed the happiness from her face. She moistened her lips. "Listen, you're okay," she assured the beekeeper, surprised to realize that it was true. "And no matter what happens, just remember none of it was your fault, all right?" If Annie Bowen could just remember those words, maybe it wouldn't hurt too much when she woke up tomorrow and realized it had been a bad fit after all.

At ten forty-five, with Annie safely in bed, Cat dropped her purse, backpack, and the patchwork quilt out of the porch window. She'd had to peel the quilt out from under Peaches, who gave her a drowsy, reproachful look. "Go back to sleep, pooch," Cat directed. "And just because I'm leaving, don't take it personally, okay? You're a good old mutt and your mistress isn't too bad either, but this is the way it has to be, got it?"

The old dog struggled to sit upright in the middle of the bed and studied her with faded, solemn eyes. Cat, one leg already hooked over the windowsill, crawled back into the room and perched on the edge of the bed.

"I'd invite you to come along, Peaches, but I don't think you'd like it very well on Harley Street," she whispered, and kissed the silky spot between his ears. He still

74

smelled strong, and if she planned to stick around Sweet-berry, one of the first things she'd do would be to give him a bath.

"You'd never get used to the noise," she explained, "and there are too many cars. Hey, you might even get killed. But living way out here in the boonies isn't my bag either, see. That's why we gotta part company."

Cat realized with regret that she'd forgotten to ask Annie for a picture of Peaches. Too bad; she'd have liked one just to take out of her wallet now and then. No way could she do anything about it now, though, being due to meet Hooter in ten minutes.

"Lay down, like a good boy, and go back to sleep," Cat urged. "When morning comes, you'll forget about me, and I'll bet Annie gets another girl real soon who'll be lots better company for you than I could ever be."

Peaches, ghost-colored in the starlight that filled the porch, wasn't convinced. Finally, Cat pulled his front legs gently out from under him and pressed him down onto the bed. She patted his lumpy, arthritic shoulder, sorry that it was the last time she would do so.

"Sweet dreams," she crooned in his ear. "Don't think about it anymore, okay?" Wasn't it what she so often advised herself? Don't think about what you're doing, Cat, she told herself, *don't think don't think*.

Cat gave the old dog three quick farewell pats, didn't look back at him again, and crawled nimbly through the window. The drop to the ground was even easier than she expected it to be. She scooped her stuff up and hurried across the weedy field toward the abandoned house. There was a sliver of moon in the western sky and nearby a bright star that last night Annie had said was the planet Venus. In the moonlight, the weeds looked almost pretty,

75

and once in a while a firefly winked above the nodding heads of the purple thistles.

What if Hooter didn't show up? Cat wondered suddenly. No, she was quite sure that he would. The glimmer of awakening in the dark eyes behind those tinted lenses this afternoon assured her that he finally understood exactly what the Look meant. She felt warm all over, knowing what it would be like when his arms circled her, when his lips on her neck were as hot as a brand. His voice in her ear would soon be husky with desire, and his words would be the ones she craved to hear: "You're special . . . I think I love you . . . you're different from any girl I ever knew."

When Cat came around the corner of the porch she saw Hooter's old green truck parked under the oak tree. She went quickly to it and peered inside. No Hooter. She paused, her hand on the truck door, the metal cool beneath her fingers. A voice called softly from the porch steps.

"Over here," Hooter whispered. "You're late. I was beginning to think you'd changed your mind about what you wanted to tell me."

His reminder unsettled Cat; she'd almost forgotten that little fib. She was glad it was dark and that he couldn't see the surprise on her face. "I didn't change my mind," she promised him in a voice as soft as his, and lowered herself onto the porch step beside him.

"So?" Hooter inquired after a moment's silence. "What is it?"

"Well, actually, I wanted to see you again. That's all."

"That's all?" He seemed a little annoyed. "How come you couldn't see me tomorrow when you come to 4-H practice?"

"I never said I was going to come to your practice," Cat pointed out. "Anyway, I'm not even going to be here to-morrow."

"How come? Where're you gonna be?"

"Back where I belong," Cat explained. "All this outdoor stuff—bees and wondering about that new queen and if she's doing what she's supposed to—hey, that's not my style, y'know?"

Hooter clamped his hands between his knees and leaned forward in the darkness. Cat could see moonlight reflected on the bridge of his nose and glinting off the steel arm of his aviator glasses. "I figured you liked it here," he observed mournfully. "And Annie's a neat old gal in my opinion."

"You reminded me yourself that she doesn't like to be called old," Cat purred. She inched closer to him on the step, near enough to feel the warmth of his arm against hers.

Hooter chuckled. "I was only teasing her that morning in the kitchen," he admitted. "Annie's about the same age as my Aunt Winifred. She doesn't like to be called old either."

A conversation like this one could go on all night and never lead anyplace interesting, Cat realized. She leaned forward too, so that her elbow actually touched Hooter's. "You want to go inside the house?" she whispered.

"Go in the house?" he echoed. Cat couldn't tell if he was eager or scared. She slipped her hand around his elbow and stroked the smooth skin on the inside of his arm.

"Sure. Nobody will see us." She leaned closer and brushed her lips against his ear. "Tomorrow I'll be gone, so you don't need to worry about me hanging on you or anything like that. Nobody'll ever bug you about me because nobody'll ever know."

Hooter laughed nervously. "Are you trying to seduce me or something?" He tried to joke. Cat was surprised that he even knew the word.

"Sure," she admitted lightly. She rose off the step, laced her fingers in his, and led him through the door into the empty old house. Moonlight fell in faint silver blocks on the floor, and she trailed Annie's quilt behind her.

"Uh, I'm not so sure this is a real good idea—" Hooter objected.

"Sure it is," she murmured. "Like I told you, I'll be gone when morning comes. We've only got tonight. Tonight we can do anything we want. . . ." She let her words trail tantalizingly away in the darkness.

Somewhat to her amazement, Hooter finally draped his arms around her shoulders. Instead of pulling her close and branding her face and neck with kisses, however, he began to rock her gently from side to side.

"Cat—I bet that isn't your real name, is it?" he whispered into her hair.

"No more than yours is really Hooter," she countered, and laughed in spite of herself. If you laughed, it meant nothing very romantic was happening.

"Mine's Harold. I'm named after my dad. What's yours?"

"No wonder they call you Hooter."

"So what's yours?" he asked again.

"Cathleen." Cat didn't tell him it was Gwendolyn Kincaid's middle name.

"I don't think you're really much like a cat," Hooter breathed against her cheek. "You seem more like a kitten to me."

78

"Oh, but kittens can scratch," Cat teased in her silkiest voice, and trailed her fingernails down his spine. She pressed herself close against him, fitting herself expertly into the curve of his body.

"Don't, Cat," Hooter cautioned. "I'm not a piece of machinery with on and off switches. If we keep on, we might end up—"

Cat leaped back. "Hey, what's wrong with you?" she snarled. "Don't do a Boy Scout number on me, okay? You know why you met me here tonight—you knew it was a good excuse to be alone together—and you knew it wasn't because we intended to play Monopoly!" She reached out and tried to pull him roughly forward.

Hooter didn't budge; moving him was like trying to uproot a tree. "All right, forget it!" Cat hissed. "You think you're the only fish in the ocean? Listen, buddy, I know dozens of guys who'd be more'n happy to trade places with you!"

Hooter caught her with a firm hand on her shoulder as Cat flung herself past him. "Don't go, Cat," he said. "I mean it. Don't leave Sweetberry. Let's face it. You wouldn't be here in the first place if somebody hadn't figured you needed a person like Annie."

"A person like Annie!" Cat mimicked in a smirky voice. "What do you know about what I need? All you know anything about is that crappy head, heart, hands, health stuff. You don't know anything about what's happened to me, what people have done to me. Okay, so Annie said you were sweet, but cavities this chick doesn't need!"

"I think maybe you've done a lot of things to yourself, Cat," Hooter observed quietly.

"Done things to myself?" Cat was incredulous. He

thought some of the things that had happened were *her* fault? She reached back to punch him, but Hooter caught her wrist in midblow.

"You've got a chance here, Cat," he insisted, "but all you want to do is muck it up. You want to get it on with me, and then you want to hit the road like it didn't matter. You don't want to take a chance on maybe being a friend."

"You turkey! When I want your advice, I'll ask for it. All right?"

"You say 4-H is crap, but you don't know anything about it. You're too chicken even to come to practice with me."

"Keep your free counseling for someone who needs it worse'n I do, Dr. Lewis."

"You could even learn to square-dance sometime."

"Only people with square heads go square dancing. Next you'll tell me I oughta go back to school."

"You dropped out?"

"What if I did? I didn't belong at Jefferson any more than I belong out here in the boonies with an old ditz who's turned on by bees."

"There aren't many jobs you can get without an education," Hooter warned. "You'll end up slinging hamburgers the rest of your life."

"Oh, I can always make money," Cat purred suggestively.

"Yeah? Doing what?" Hooter wanted to know.

But Cat decided she'd already heard and said enough. "I gotta get going," she informed him, and headed for the door.

"So you're really going to do it?"

"Believe it, fella. I've been here about a week too long already."

Hooter held his wrist up to catch the moonlight on the face of his watch. "It's almost midnight," he reported. "You don't have a car, and I'm not taking you anywhere. There's no way you can leave tonight."

"Just watch me," Cat invited. On the porch she flicked her thumb under his nose. "I'll start hitching as soon as I get to the highway."

"Hitching's like asking for it. People have ended up dead in ditches doing that."

"*I* haven't," Cat boasted, and scooped her gear off the steps of the porch.

Hooter grabbed her again and when she tried to twist away he only held her harder. "Listen, I'll make you a deal," he offered, "one you won't be able to refuse."

"What kind of deal?" Cat demanded suspiciously.

"If you promise to stay here two more weeks, I'll take you anywhere you want to go. I'll crank up the Green Machine, and if you want a ride back to the city, that's where I'll take you. But only if you stay two more weeks."

"Jeez! I bet you really *were* a Boy Scout!" Cat sighed wearily.

"Actually, I was. I made Eagle Scout when I was fifteen; no guy around here ever did that before."

"Saint Harold the Good. Pardon me, I think I'm going to be sick."

"Excuse me, madam. We don't allow any upchuck on the premises," Hooter said in a snotty butler's voice. Cat hated to laugh but couldn't hold back a tired giggle.

"Okay, you win for now." She groaned. "I'll stay two

81

more weeks—and afterward you'll take me anywhere I want to go, right?"

"You got it."

"How about Florida?"

"That might require further discussion," Hooter admitted, and let his arm fall lightly across her shoulders.

How can this be happening? Cat wondered. They hadn't done anything, but she felt almost happy in spite of it. The weight of Hooter's arm on her shoulders wasn't full of passion, and she didn't have a single hickey on her neck, so how come she felt glad nothing had gone according to plan?

"So I'll see you tomorrow, okay?" Hooter persevered. "About seven-thirty. I gotta be on time at the hall, so you better be ready."

"Whatever," Cat agreed softly. Hooter rapped her lightly on the arm with his knuckles, then jumped into his truck. He didn't turn on the headlights until he got to the highway, and although Cat waved good-bye, she was sure he hadn't noticed. She went back into the house and rescued Annie's quilt from the floor. She slung her purse and backpack over her arm and headed across the silver field toward the darkened bungalow.

Peaches stirred sleepily from his place in the middle of the bed when she crawled through the still-open window. "Shhhhh," Cat whispered, "don't give me away." She heard his tail thump once in a conspiratorial greeting, and peeled off her jeans and shirt, mindful of how good she still smelled and how smooth her skin felt. She pulled the sheet up to her neck, and Peaches rolled his weight comfortably against her flank.

Hey, is this me? Cat wondered. The moon edged behind the row of trees that lined Annie's driveway, and darkness filled the porch. Cat turned, adjusted her bones, and looped an arm around Peaches's shoulder. Can I finally afford to quit being tough and dangerous? she asked herself, but was asleep before she could figure out the answer.

8

Just knowing that at seven-thirty Hooter was coming by to pick her up in the Green Machine made the day different from the moment Cat opened her eyes.

Was it because she'd never had a date before but now she was going to? she wondered, staring dreamily at the ceiling of the bedroom on the porch. There'd been lots of guys, of course, the kind a person met on street corners or at the Adult Arts bookstore or down in the park, but nobody had ever picked her up from the place where she lived and taken her somewhere else. Maybe after practice she and Hooter would linger in the cab of the Green Machine, and he would reach across the seat and just hold her hand. She'd lace her fingers in his, and they wouldn't do anything else, not even kiss. Maybe later, on a different date, that might happen. It might even make her feel like a person whose real name was Cathleen.

Cat washed the breakfast dishes without being asked and decided that, with Annie working at the table nearby, it would be a good time to tell the beekeeper about the date. She wished, though, that she'd never laid all that stuff about the big *P* word on Annie. What if, remembering the things she'd been told, Annie now refused to let her go anywhere with Hooter? What if Annie freaks out about what I might try to get on with Hooter? Cat worried.

There was only one way to find out for sure. Cat cleared her throat. "Hooter's going to pick me up at seven-thirty," she murmured casually, as if the news were nothing special.

"No kidding!" Annie exclaimed. "Where're you two going?"

"Noplace real exciting," Cat murmured, and hoped she sounded blasé about the whole caper. "He's gotta practice his square-dance stuff. I'm only going along, you know, to watch."

"I think that's kind of neat, Cat." Annie sounded pleased. What? No stern lectures, no frantic warning about not fooling around with a boy who was seventeen and sweet?

"Aren't you afraid that I might mess around with—I mean, after I told you all that stuff about what I've done with guys, I figured you might think I'd try to—"

"And maybe you won't," Annie interrupted. She stood at the table, crumbling chunks of honeycomb into a large container, which filled the whole kitchen with a light, flowery odor. Suddenly Annie cocked her head and flashed Cat a shrewd, questioning glance.

"Is it my imagination, Cat, or do I get the feeling you're not real comfortable about going out with Hooter tonight?" she asked.

How had she picked up on that so fast? Cat wondered,

amazed. She tried to shrug off the question and wrung out the dishrag without answering right away. "I don't think— what I mean is, I'm not too sure I'll fit in very well with Hooter's friends," she admitted finally.

"See, maybe it'll be just like when I started at Jefferson after my Gram died and we had to move to the project. I never found a way to belong there, and the longer I stayed, the worse it got." Cat was surprised to hear herself putting the pain of those days into such ordinary words; she'd never confessed any of this to anyone before—not to Mom (who didn't seem to care) and most especially not to Mrs. Allen (who cared too much).

"Maybe you just ought to be yourself, Cat," Annie advised quietly, resting her large brown hands on the lip of the plastic container. "Who you are seems plenty good enough to me."

Cat felt a burning sting at the bridge of her nose, the kind she always got just before she started to cry. Jeez! She didn't want to cry. It'd make her feel so weak and wimpy and needful, the way she'd felt for so long after she'd moved away from Gram's house, the way she felt until she became a leopard. She'd better change the subject, Cat decided; to talk about those days at Jefferson was like probing a wound that refused to heal.

"What're you doing with that junk?" Cat muttered brusquely, watching Annie break up pieces of honeycomb. "I thought you were going into town today."

"Decided to go later in the week," Annie replied. "Today seemed like a good day to render honey from old combs. Later, maybe you'd like to help me make some candles. Until you've eaten a Thanksgiving turkey or a Christmas ham by the light of a beeswax candle, Cat, you haven't lived! As the candle burns down, the wax releases

86

the smell of all the flowers the bees have visited during the summer—clover and basswood and roses—all mixed into one heavenly smell!"

Listening to Annie, Cat almost smiled. Only yesterday, she marveled, she'd never have believed she might still be at Sweetberry when the holidays rolled around. She stepped up to the table and began to help Annie crumble chunks of old honeycomb. Now, the wish not to run away anymore, the suspicion that she might be able to find a place to be herself, not somebody she'd invented, made Annie's little kitchen seem like—Cat searched her mind for just the right word—well, almost like home.

At six-thirty, Cat washed her face, patted it dry, and inspected herself in the mirror above the chipped sink in Annie's bathroom. She smoothed on some moisturizer. She seemed pale, unlike the Cat she'd grown so accustomed to seeing. She hesitated, remembering Annie's advice just to be herself.

Somehow, just being herself didn't seem quite good enough for an evening that was so important, Cat decided, and quickly smoothed on some Aztec Bronze makeup. Next came eye shadow that was brushed on well beyond the corners of her eyes, then eyeliner in heavy strokes, followed by a first coat of mascara. When the first coat had dried, she applied a second and a third, until at last her lashes were as thick and stiff as a doll's. She polished her cheeks with blusher, then painted her full lips with gloss.

There. The mask that had taken shape in the mirror was the face that belonged to the girl Cat was sure she knew best. The eyes that stared unblinkingly into her own were cool and green; the hair that fell to her shoulders was inky, although yesterday she'd noticed that the roots at her temples were getting lighter, which meant she'd soon have to get some new dye.

Satisfied, Cat pulled on her black jeans and her black T-shirt with the red rose. Annie had washed them only this morning, so both were nice and tight. Cat turned sideways to examine her profile in the mirror on the closet door in the hallway. No lie, she really did have a super bod. She paused. Was the shirt just a little *too* tight? Maybe she should—but then she heard the crunch of tires on the gravel outside and stopped only long enough to ram her bare feet into her black boots, throw her fringed black leather bag over her shoulder, and dash out into the yard before Hooter had a chance to climb out of the Green Machine.

What Cat saw through the windshield of Hooter's truck froze the happy smile that pulled at the corners of her mouth.

Shirl, the squirrel, sat right next to Hooter, a lot closer than a girl who wasn't supposed to be a girlfriend needed to. She wore hardly a single speck of makeup and looked as scrubbed and shining as somebody's ten-year-old kid sister. She had on a blouse of yellow-and-white checkered material with enormous puffy sleeves and a scooped neckline trimmed with eyelet embroidery. Cat hated everything she saw.

Hooter leaped cheerfully out of the truck and bounded forward. Cat took a single step backward. "What's *she* doing here?" she hissed before he could say a word. "I thought it was going to be just you and me tonight. I thought we were going to have—"

To have a date, she'd almost said, then bit her tongue. Actually, Hooter had never said that, Cat realized with helpless fury. He'd only asked if she wanted to come and watch a 4-H square-dance practice. Period. *She* was the one who'd made a mistake; she'd written the wrong scenario again, just as she'd daydreamed that Annie's farmhouse might be the picturebook kind.

"Shirl needed a ride tonight," Hooter explained, unperturbed. "She's got a car, but the battery's been dead for a week, and she hasn't saved up for a new one yet. We can all go to practice together, okay?" His fingers (the ones she'd dreamed of lacing with her own) were warm and firm on her wrist, and Cat allowed herself to be propelled toward the passenger's side of the Green Machine. She'd been an idiot to have pictured herself sitting alone with Hooter, to have been happy holding his hand and not doing anything else, Cat decided wrathfully.

"Cat, this is Shirl," Hooter said when he opened the door of the truck. "Shirl, meet Cat."

Shirl smiled sweetly out of her bare, scrubbed face, and Cat recognized all too well the look in the other girl's eyes. Dig that crazy makeup! those innocent blue eyes exclaimed. Where'd she ever find an outfit like that? those raised eyebrows inquired.

I'm an outsider again, Cat realized suddenly. I don't belong here any more than I belonged at Jefferson. Once, she'd worn black nylons and a pair of spike-heeled shoes to school; she'd gotten them from the Used Goods Galore store. The shoes even fit well and were so gorgeous with their rhinestone buckles. Everybody at school, though, had stared at her as if she'd just arrived on a spaceship from Mars. Not a single person ever said the shoes were pretty, except for the janitor who, even when he told her so, looked at her sort of queerly.

That same week, somebody had sprayed her locker with four-letter words, real ugly ones, in bright red paint. Guys could be like that, Cat had thought—but when the culprits were caught a couple days later, they turned out to be Madge Beasley and SuAnn Mitchell, who belonged to the Booster Club and wouldn't have been caught dead using such words out loud.

A familiar desire for revenge suddenly took hold of Cat. "Hi," she heard herself murmur in her silkiest voice to Shirl, who scooted ever farther across the seat and huddled so close to Hooter that she was almost on his lap. She looks as if she just remembered she saw my picture on a "Most Wanted" circular at the post office, Cat realized bitterly.

But she's got freckles and a flat chest, Cat noted smugly, and propped herself, full-chested and stony-faced, against the door of the Green Machine. She stared hard at the road, and permitted herself a tiny, wicked smile. Hooter should've warned her that he was dragging Shirl along, right? But he hadn't; in a way, he had betrayed her, had made a fool out of her.

Okay, buddy, Cat vowed silently, just wait till we get to your dumb 4-H hall. I'll put on a show for you that everybody will talk about long after Cat Kincaid has blown this crummy place. Just you wait, buster; I will, no lie.

When they arrived at the Channing County 4-H hall, it was to discover that some of the square-dance groups were already practicing their routines. As soon as Hooter appeared, a gray-haired man wearing a straw hat approached, an agitated expression on his sweating face.

"I thought you might not show up, Hoot," he moaned, and mopped his shiny forehead with a red cowboy-style kerchief. "Do you think you could call for me tonight? The wife and I hafta run over to Plainview for a couple of hours, and I'd sure like to leave early. If you could just—"

Cat hung back, listened coolly to the arrangements that were being made, and with slitted eyes studied the boys and girls who filled the room. The girls all wore the same sort of outfit that Shirl had on, a dress with snug bodice, puffy sleeves, and a skirt held out with many crisp white crinoline petticoats. The guys wore blue jeans, boots, and western-style kerchiefs with their shirts.

As she looked at everyone else, however, Cat realized they were staring back at her. Suddenly, the red rose on her T-shirt seemed to burn a hole through her heart, and her jeans felt so snug that she could hardly take a deep breath. In this roomful of scrubbed, down-home types, she knew she must look like a chick straight out of an X-rated movie. There was only one thing she could do now: she stood as tall as she could, propped a fist on her cranked-out hip, and boldly returned the stares. The girls all reminded her of Annie's dumb chickens, clucking, ready to squawk and run, so Cat made it a point to stare only at the boys.

"Hey, who's that dude over there?" she whispered to Shirl, and pointed to the only interesting-looking guy in the whole hall.

"That's J-J Irving," Shirl chirped sweetly. "He's a year older than the rest of us on account of he didn't have enough credits to graduate last year when he should've. Mostly he goes around with my sister Merrilee."

Cat felt J-J Irving's glance slide over her shirt, jeans, and come to rest on the petals of her rose. In return, she treated him to the Look. It was plain that he picked up right away on what it meant.

91

"You mean he *used* to go with dear old Merrilee," Cat purred in Shirl's ear. Once you'd made up your mind to get even, you could always figure out a way to do it, Cat mused. Hooter had hauled Shirl the squirrel along on what ought to have been a date; okay, then she'd find a date of her own, Cat vowed.

Before she could make a move on J-J, however, Hooter started to call the squares, and everyone began to dance. It looked as if it might have been fun, and Cat especially liked the one they danced to the tune of "You Picked a Fine Time to Leave Me, Lucille." All that dancing, though, made it hard to touch base with J-J, and it was only when the practice was all finished that Cat could sidle up to him.

"Hey, J-J." She greeted him knowingly in her smoothest voice.

"How'd you know my name?" he asked, grinning. He was taller than Hooter and had sassy, wise eyes. There was a dimple in his chin, and Cat realized that she would've noticed him even if she hadn't been determined to pay Hooter back.

"I asked, that's how." She didn't have time to futz around and would get right to the point, Cat decided. "Listen, J-J, I need a ride home," she purred. "How about giving me a lift?"

"Wow, lady, you don't waste time!" J-J marveled and smiled wider. He shot a wary glance in Hooter's direction and added, "But what's Mr. Clean gonna think about this? I saw you come in with him, so—"

"So that doesn't necessarily mean I gotta go home with him, right? Nobody's got me on a leash, y'know."

J-J drove a truck too, a much newer and nicer one than the Green Machine, Cat was pleased to note, and in the glow of the dash lights J-J Irving looked even cuter than he had at the 4-H hall. He fished expertly in the breast pocket of his blue-checked shirt for cigarettes and handed one to her.

"You're a real lifesaver," she breathed huskily, and when he held the glowing tip of the dash lighter for her, she steadied his hand with her own. She leaned back, inhaled deeply, and let the smoke out slowly. She gestured with the cigarette. "I'd almost forgotten how good one of these could taste!" She sighed.

"I got something under the seat that'll taste even better," J-J murmured, "providing you don't mind warm beer, that is."

"Listen, warm beer and a cigarette are the best offers I've had since I got to this stupid place," Cat assured him.

"You must be one of those girls old Annie Bowen keeps at her place every now and then," J-J guessed.

"You got it. I'm leaving tonight, though. I've learned enough about bees and Boy Scouts to last me the rest of my life, no kidding." The twin beams of J-J's truck knifed the darkness, and Cat added casually, "Hey, you ever been to that old broken-down mansion near Sweetberry?"

"Yeah, a couple of times. Went there once with some guys, and we pitched a few rocks through the upstairs windows—which was real juvenile, and I'm kind of sorry now we did it."

"Want to go there tonight?" Cat murmured, snubbing her cigarette out in the ashtray, her eyes on the road. She could sense J-J inspect her profile, then with the tip of a finger he reached out to tease one of the tangled black curls that brushed her cheek. "Lady, I gotta tell you you're not much like the girls around here, if you get what I mean," he whispered.

Cat turned to smile at him with narrowed eyes. "You better believe I'm not," she promised. When J-J eased his truck into the blackness under the oak tree next to the porch of the mansion, Cat turned to him again with a sleepy, feline smile. The kiss they shared was long and deep and warmed her down to the soles of her feet. Then J-J's mouth was on her neck, and his hand against the small of her back was experienced and purposeful.

"Let's go into the house," Cat whispered huskily. J-J didn't answer, simply opened the door on his side of the truck and pulled her eagerly across the seat. Yes, Cat thought, I've decided to do this of my own free will, and it doesn't have a darn thing to do with not facing my real problems.

Cat had her hand on the rusty old doorknob when a pair of headlights illuminated the porch like searchlights from a prison watchtower. She recognized the asthmatic wheeze of the Green Machine. "Shut off those damn lights!" Cat demanded. "Whoever nominated you to be my keeper, anyway?"

Hooter didn't get out of his truck, but before he shut off its lights, Cat could see that Shirl wasn't with him. "Hey, J-J," he called through the darkness, sounding neither angry nor surprised as he greeted Merrilee's most-of-the-time boyfriend.

"Hey, Hoot," J-J replied with the same kind of measured carefulness in his voice. "What's on your mind, buddy?"

"There's something I gotta talk to Cat about," Hooter replied.

"So say it and get lost," Cat snapped balefully.

"It's kind of private," Hooter replied equivocally.

Cat felt J-J let go of her fingers. "Listen, it's no big

deal," he muttered. "I was supposed to go meet Merrilee tonight anyhow." Incensed, Cat reached out to stop him, but J-J was off the porch and back into his truck like a flash.

"Chicken!" she hollered after him as he departed.

She whirled, furious, to confront Hooter. "Okay, smart guy, what's this all about?" she yelled. "If you want to play counselor, go pick somebody who really needs it. I don't!" She could kill right now for another drag off one of J-J's cigarettes, for another thirsty pull on that can of warm beer. Cat flung herself off the porch of the old house, her purse slapping her hip as she headed across the weedy field toward Annie's bungalow, but Hooter caught up before she'd gone twenty feet.

"Okay, okay, I apologize for not telling you Shirl needed a ride tonight," he said, "but is that the end of the world? I figured it'd be just you and me too, but we can try again. We can go to a movie or something. Tomorrow night—yeah, Cat, how about doing something tomorrow night?"

"Sorry, buster, I won't be around tomorrow night," Cat informed him coldly, and kept her back turned to him.

Hooter placed a hand on each of her shoulders. "Don't go, Cat," he urged softly. "Stay here at Sweetberry. Look, what happened to you before you came here isn't any of my business, but nothing's ever going to get better if you just take a flier. It'll only get worse, right? I'm not asking you to stay for me; not for Annie, either. Stay for yourself, Cat; stay for yourself."

Cat wrenched herself free. "Forget it," she said, and knew suddenly why it had to end this way: she didn't really want to give up the old life. No, not really; that long, deep, hungry kiss with J-J had made her realize certain things were too sweet to be abandoned. No way, though, could she ever explain something like that to Mr. Clean. Cat left Hooter standing alone in the field of purple thistles. She didn't look back and didn't bother to call good-bye.

9

Although she'd bragged to Hooter about hitching, doing it at night always spooked Cat. Whenever a car pulled off the road for you in the dark, you felt a pang of relief that was followed by a rush of fear because you couldn't tell for sure who was inside until you got right up next to it.

Suppose it was a carload of young guys; that could mean a ton of fun or it could be real bad news. When she'd gone to the People's Free Clinic that time, Cat had seen a couple of chicks who'd been beat up bad, had split lips and bruised eyes and no telling what else that a person couldn't see. They'd gotten roughed up, they said, when they'd hitched their way home from the state fair and been picked up by three cute dudes who turned out to be mean and drunk. What Cat prayed to get whenever she hitched after dark was a family coming home from a trip, with maybe a couple of kids and a dog asleep in the back seat.

A light-colored car (in the dark, Cat couldn't tell if it was cream or gray) pulled onto the soft shoulder not long after she left Annie's narrow road, its taillights a pair of glowing beacons winking at her from where it'd stopped. She hesitated, crossed her fingers, then ran up alongside it. She bent quickly and peered inside. The dash lights revealed a middle-aged pair, and she heaved a sigh of relief. She jumped into the back seat, out of breath, and right away the woman in front began to lecture. It seemed to be a habit middle-aged women got into real easy.

"I told my husband, 'Ralph,' I said, 'we'd better pick up that child before somebody else does. She might never get where she's going if we don't.'" The woman turned and spoke emphatically into the cavernous darkness of the back seat. "Hitchhiking is a terribly dangerous thing to do, my dear. Hasn't anyone ever told you that?"

All the time, Cat nearly answered, smirking to herself at that word, child. Nevertheless, she murmured demurely, "Yes, ma'am, I know it is, but I really needed to get home." She made her voice small and beseeching, and as she told her story, she almost believed it herself.

"I didn't have any bus fare, see, and I figured maybe this once I'd be lucky with whoever stopped for me. I've been on vacation at my aunt's house, and all of a sudden I just got real lonesome to see my mom." The woman in the front seat was immediately sympathetic, as Cat intended she should be.

"Now doesn't that sound familiar!" the woman cried. "One summer, our daughter—our daughter's name is Beverly—went off to Kamp Koorage and got lonesome just like that. My, the phone bills we had—didn't we, Ralph?" She leaned toward her husband in the cheery glow of the dashboard panel, and they shared the memory of the giant phone bills caused by Beverly's homesickness.

Alone in the cavelike blackness of the back seat, Cat

wondered what it might have been like to have been Beverly, who had two parents who cared enough to send her to camp and were happy to pay the phone bills when she got so lonesome she had to call home every day.

When they neared the city, Mr. and Mrs. Davis—they insisted that she call them Ralph and Marjorie, and Cat told them her name was Susan St. Clare—wanted to know where she'd like to be dropped off. To have mentioned Harley Street, which was known by everyone to have a sordid reputation, would have been uncool, so Cat sweetly requested the bus stop at Folwell and Twelfth Avenue.

"I can catch a ride home from there on the B bus," she told them. "You guys have both been real nice, but I don't want to impose any more'n I already have."

"It was no imposition, Susan," Marjorie Davis assured her. "We were on our way home anyway, and it was real nice to have had your company. My, your Aunt Annie sounds like such an interesting lady, raising bees the way she does. But please, dear, promise us that you won't hitchhike anymore. Tonight you were lucky; tonight you got Ralph and me, isn't that right, Ralph?"

Ralph nodded dutifully. "You might not be so fortunate next time—am I right, Ralph?" Ralph nodded obediently. "We'd feel so dreadful if some morning we picked up the *Tribune* and read that something terrible had happened to a sweet girl named Susan St. Clare!"

"I won't do it again," Cat promised solemnly. If the name Cathleen Kincaid appeared in the paper, the Davises could heave a sigh of relief that it wasn't anyone they'd ever heard of, which made Cat feel anonymous. She wished she'd given them her real name after all.

"Tell Beverly I think she's a real lucky girl," Cat said

when she climbed out at the curb. She meant it, too: the ride with the Davises had been safe, and she'd even been able to doze off once during a lengthy account of Beverly's trip to Washington, D.C., as a student senator years ago when she was in the eleventh grade.

When Cat closed the car door, however, she saw an astonished expression on Mrs. Davis's face. In the bright lights of the street the poor woman could plainly see what her passenger looked like in black jeans, tight black shirt with a rose on it, not to mention a tangle of black corkscrew curls and an abundance of mascara. Marjorie Davis was as appalled as Shirl, the squirrel, had been.

Cat responded automatically, gave her an insulting, middle-finger gesture, and saw poor Marjorie's shocked face looking back through the rear window as the car pulled away from the curb. I didn't have to do that, Cat realized, but it was too late to take the gesture back. The taillights of the Davis car were soon lost in the confusion of traffic on Folwell, and she turned the corner and headed for Harley Street two blocks away.

It always surprised Cat to see how much difference two blocks could make: on Folwell and Twelfth, there were nice shops, boutiques, and nifty eateries with stained-glass lamps lighting their smoked windows. Harley Street belonged to another world: instead of fancy shops there were a succession of used-clothes stores, pawnshops, and X-rated bookstores. Cat hesitated on the corner, wondering if she'd run into anybody she knew. She didn't, so she headed down to the middle of the block between Eleventh and Twelfth Avenue to Davey Gibson's apartment above the Used Goods Galore store.

The stairway to the third floor was dimly lit and smelled strongly of garbage and urine. Cat sidestepped an overflowing sack of empty beer and wine bottles on the second landing. If they were some Davey had collected and intended to sell, he'd sure been dumb to have left 'em right where somebody else could put the snatch on 'em. Cat grabbed up the sack and hauled it up to the third floor; if it turned out the bottles weren't his, she'd go ahead and sell 'em herself.

When Cat got to number 312, she tried the door. It was locked. Davey usually locked it when he was sleeping off a big one, which was bad because lately he'd been mixing pills and booze together, which really laid him out. She knocked. She put her ear to the door but couldn't hear anything going on inside. She pounded harder; boy, he must've blasted himself into outer space this time.

When she banged the third time, a door across the hall flew open, and a fat man with three days' worth of stubble on his greasy face peered out.

"Give it up, you little witch!" he yelled. "You ain't gonna rouse anybody in there. The cops busted into that place four days ago. It's for rent now. Your buddy's gone."

"Davey's gone?"

"You heard me! Now get lost, or I'll call the cops on you, too."

"Okay, okay. I'm going. Only d'you know where he went?"

"Wherever they take crazy people. He was off his rocker. Didn't know who he was or where he was at. That apartment smelled like a pile of dead cats when they opened it up. Maggots in the hamburger on the table, somebody said. Now you got five minutes before I call the cops again." He slammed his door hard, leaving Cat alone with her gear and the sackful of empty bottles still in her arms.

The windows in Davey's apartment had been painted shut and couldn't be opened anymore; it was true that if you didn't take care of things in there, it got pretty smelly. The sheets on the three beds in the apartment were always gray and stiff. The only time they were washed, Cat suspected, was when she did them herself down at the Laundromat on the corner.

Davey's place had always been safe, though; he'd never hit on her or tried to get it on with her. Once, he'd called her Little Sister and only smiled when she called herself Cat. What she'd like to do now, though, was really chew his butt for having messed up her plans. The dim yellow light in the hallway suddenly made everything look bleak and hopeless, so Cat set the sack of bottles on the floor near the landing and hurried back down the stairs. What she didn't need was Mr. Fat Face hollering for the cops again.

Outside, she leaned against the darkened window of the Used Goods Galore store. She'd counted on a meal of beans and bread at Davey's. He always kept cans of beans around because they could never go bad, but you had to check the bread to make sure it didn't have green fuzz growing on it. Jeez! It was too late to go down to the park; she'd learned her lesson on that score. To get to the Hideout, though, she'd have to walk through the park first, so that was out too.

Cat hooked her thumbs in her belt loops. She'd have to go lock herself in the john down at the Laundromat; you were better off if you locked yourself in, though still not 100 percent safe. Briefly, she considered calling Floss. Naw, that darn kid of hers cried too much, though it always bothered Cat when Floss put a few drops of booze into its bottle to keep it from whining. Angie? Forget it;

she cruised the streets now, and you never knew when she might haul some dude home.

Cat hunched her shoulders. There was one place left, of course, where she might be able to crash for a couple of nights. Not that she intended for it ever to be a permanent thing.

She could go home.

Hadn't she already told Ralph and poor, shocked Marjorie that she'd catch the B bus? Sure. All right, she'd just—then from the tail of her eye Cat saw a man approach her from across the street. He wasn't a scuzzball like most of the Harley Street regulars; he was clean, had a suit on, wore a nervous expression, and studied her expectantly.

Cat knew exactly what was on his mind. He was a nice guy from the suburbs who'd come downtown looking for some action. If you stood around on Harley Street, this was bound to happen. Somebody would assume you were there because you were willing to sell your bod, that for twenty bucks you'd do all kinds of kinky stuff.

She raced around the corner and headed back to Folwell. Her eyes felt red and dry; her lips were chapped; her stomach complained noisily, and she fantasized a can of beans from Davey's cupboard. She stopped to fish two one-dollar bills from her jeans. She'd need change; bus drivers had been held up so often that finally the bus company put signs on the fare boxes reading Correct Fare Only. The ride out to the project was seventy-five cents; she'd have enough to come back downtown tomorrow. Cat ducked into the Steak Emporium, got change, and got back on the street just in time to catch the B.

As she rode out to the project on the nearly deserted bus, Cat reflected on how weird it'd be to go home. Not that the apartment was really home; it was merely the place Mom had moved to after Gram died. It was Gram's house that had been a real home, but lately Cat had a hard time remembering exactly what it had looked like. Perhaps when you became a different person, gave yourself a new name, you had to give up everything that had belonged to that other person's past, even the memories.

One thing Cat did remember, though, was how quickly Mom fell apart after the funeral. When Gram was alive, the old lady had done everything: had a job, cooked, cleaned, cut grass, in spite of the fact that she was no bigger around than a matchstick and that the veins on her thin arms and legs stood out like dark ropes under her skin.

"I'm as strong as a horse," she boasted, and on the day she died, that's what she was like, a thin old horse that just keeled over in its traces. Cat had been there in the kitchen when it happened. Gram didn't go down hard, just sort of slumped over in her chair, and only when she was on the floor did Cat realize she couldn't have weighed more than ninety pounds.

Mom had started to cry right away, and it seemed to Cat that she didn't stop for months. On the day of Gram's death, it was Mrs. Spetzler from next door who'd had to come over and call the ambulance. It was a stroke, the medics said. You ought to be glad, they added; it's lots better this way than being a vegetable in some nursing home. Glad? Cat still wondered how you could be glad when somebody you loved had just died.

Cat got off the bus at Fifty-sixth Street and walked two blocks to the project. Low-income housing, it was called. It reminded Cat a lot more of a rabbit hutch, with cages inside filled with people who were stacked on top of other people. Tonight, there was a light on in 272A, which was a big relief. Mom had never liked to go to bed early, and for once Cat was glad. She hoped, though, that Mom would be alone, that one of her boyfriends wouldn't still be there, all mush-mouthed from having drunk beer ever since he got off work.

She knocked timidly at the door. How many other people had to knock at the front door of their own homes? she wondered. Cat heard footsteps on the other side and tensed herself. Let it be Mom, she prayed, but when the door opened she found herself staring at someone she'd never seen before.

"Is my mom here?" she croaked. Her voice was still as tiny as it'd been in the hallway outside of Davey's apartment. It was the voice of a person who was weak and scared, and Cat despised it.

The man stared at her. "Your mom?" he repeated, as blank as a post, then bellowed over his shoulder, "Hey, Gwen! There's some kid out here who's asking for her mother. You been keeping secrets from me?" He guffawed as if it were some huge joke.

When Mom came out of the kitchen, Cat could plainly see that nothing had changed. Had she been born in that old red bathrobe, for God's sake? And wouldn't a regular mother have started screaming her head off right away, yelling, "Where've you been, you damn kid? I've been worried sick about you—and what've you done to your hair?"

Mom didn't say any of those things. She just slumped in the doorway, her hands in the pockets of her robe, looking pale and tired. How could a person be tired all the time when the only things she ever did were smoke and watch the soaps?

"Hi, Mom," Cat said, grateful for the hard note that had crept back into her voice. "Listen, I gotta have a place to crash tonight. Something's happened to Davey, so I need—"

"Davey? Davey who?" her mother asked tonelessly.

Cat was startled. Of course Mom didn't know anything about Davey, not who he was or where he lived or how important he'd been these past months. "He's just a guy I know," Cat grumbled. "He got sick, though, and had to give up the place he was living in, so now I gotta have—"

Mom glanced at the man standing in the middle of the living room. "Is it okay with you, Arnie?" she inquired meekly.

"Lord, Gwen, don't ask me!" he objected loudly. His hair was red, but his mustache was brownish and had yellow streaks in it, which made it look dirty. "She's your kid, Gwen, not mine! If she belonged to me, though, I sure wouldn't want her traipsing around the streets at this hour." Cat waited for her mother to flush with embarrassment, but no bright pink spots appeared on her mother's cheeks.

"Hey, it's only for one night." Cat snapped at him, hating to sound as if she were begging. "I'll be gone by noon tomorrow. It's not like I intend to stay permanently, so chill out, okay?"

Arnie stepped aside as Cat stalked past him on her way toward her old bedroom. "How come you never mentioned you had a kid, Gwen?" he demanded, but Cat noticed that he didn't sound mad. As she passed by, he clumsily tried to be friendly and tugged at a strand of her hair. "She's not a bad-looking kid, but it looks to me like some wise guy stuck her head in an inkwell!"

Oh, sure, Cat thought, I know the type. He's trying to

be a nice guy now, but the first time Mom's got her back turned, he'll be Mr. Fast Hands. First it's my hair, next time it'll be the rest of me. He wouldn't be the first one; most of Mom's boyfriends had been the same way. Cat opened the door to her bedroom and slammed it shut behind her. She fumbled for the light switch.

The room looked as if it hadn't been vacuumed or dusted since she left. Cat tried to open the window, but the crank was stuck, and she succeeded only in shaking dust out of the curtains and making herself sneeze. It was stuffy and too warm in the room, but at least it was safe. On second thought, maybe not safe enough; she went back to the door and turned the lock before she climbed into bed.

When she stretched out, Cat was surprised to find that the bed seemed a lot more spacious than she remembered. She lay in the middle, spread her arms wide on either side, and realized why it seemed so roomy: she didn't have to scrunch over to one side to make room for Peaches.

Peaches. Sweetberry. Annie. Hooter. Perhaps she'd only imagined such people. She pressed her thumbs against her eyeballs and realized again how starved she was. It was Davey's fault: she'd counted on being able to count on him. Instead, he'd screwed up, had gotten hauled away by the cops; there was no telling when he might show up again or what kind of shape he'd be in when he did.

Floss and Angie couldn't be banked on anymore either; forget both of them. Well, she'd just have to hit Mom up for some cash in the morning. She'd need enough to go rent a room for herself down on Harley Street; she'd need a place to lay low in for a while. Eventually she'd have to

107

get herself a job. Maybe the Used Goods Galore store needed somebody; she'd try it first thing in the morning.

Cat reached out in the darkness and stroked the empty space on either side of herself. She wished she'd remembered to ask for a picture of Peaches; right now it'd be nice if she could turn on the light and look at it for a few moments. At night, that old dog had been a kind of anchor, his weight on the bed so solid, his breathing so regular and easy. Cat sighed. In the morning she'd decide what she was going to do next. In the morning decisions were always easier to make.

10

Cat woke, face down in her old bed. The dusty pillow seemed unfamiliar, and she rolled over fast, scared, her legs tangled in the sheet. Panic made her heart hammer loudly in her chest. She stared at the ceiling. Light filtered through the soiled yellow curtains at the window, and she remembered: she was home, had returned to the place she'd vowed never to come back to.

From the living room came the sound of a man's voice, then the muffled closing of a door and steps receding down the hall. Cat glanced at the clock on the nightstand; it was almost eleven. She'd promised to be gone by noon; she jumped up, grabbed her clothes, and unlocked the bedroom door.

She peered into the living room to make sure whatshisface—Arnie?—was really gone, and discovered that her first impression about Mom last night had been right on target: she hadn't changed at all. There she was, camped out on the couch, cigarette smoke encircling her head like a pale blue halo, listening to somebody on a talk show complain that the problem with women was that they didn't assert themselves enough.

Tell me about it, Cat thought, and headed for the bathroom. After she'd showered and fixed her face, she padded in sock feet through the living room into the kitchen. This wasn't a morning for the traditional cigarette/ Pepsi/candy-bar breakfast, but there wasn't much to eat in the fridge, only half a dozen eggs, a loaf of bread that felt stale when she squeezed the wrapper, and a half-empty carton of skim milk. Cat scrambled two eggs, poured some milk into a chipped jelly glass, and was surprised when Mom switched off the TV and came into the kitchen herself.

Listen, if she gets on my case one little bit, I'm really gonna let her have it! Cat vowed. But her mother simply poured herself another cup of coffee, lit another cigarette, and sat silently on the opposite side of the table. If she doesn't want to talk to me, why'd she come out here? Cat wondered bitterly, and shoveled eggs into her mouth. She watched her mother snub out the cigarette on the edge of her saucer and realized that she was trying to figure out a way to begin a conversation in which things that were hard to say were going to be said.

"I have to talk to you, Cathy," Gwen Kincaid began slowly.

Cat saw her mother study the handles on the kitchen drawers as if they might be able to give her some tips on how to proceed with the conversation. She doesn't know I'm called Cat now, Cat realized. She'd never known Davey, didn't know anything about Floss or Angie either. What we are is strangers to each other; maybe we always have been. Mom doesn't even know about Sweetberry,

Cat reflected, but before she could bring up the subject, her mother touched on it herself.

"First of all, Cathy, I suppose I'd better ask where you've been all this time. The last thing I heard, you were living with some people named Wilson." Her mother detached her gaze from the drawer handles, and Cat realized with surprise that her large, reproachful eyes were as green as her own. "How come you never called?" Her mother's voice was plaintive.

"My whereabouts sure never bothered you before," Cat snapped back. "There were lots of times I was gone—jeez, one, two, three nights in a row—and you never asked then. So what if it stretched out to a couple months or even longer? Gram never would've put up with that crap, but you know something? I think *you* were relieved! Yeah; see, with me gone, you never had to worry about any of your guys looking my way." Cat paused in her tirade. "Anyway, didn't old Mrs. Allen call you and tell you where the welfare dumped me this time?"

Her mother's green eyes were blank. "Well, if it's anything to you, they stuck me on a bee farm. Can you believe it? A woman named Annie runs the place. She's got a dog named Peaches, and she makes her living selling honey."

"Did you like it there?" Cat was certain she detected a note of hope in her mother's voice.

"What's to like about bees?" Cat yelled, enraged. "I'm a street person! No way do I belong out in the boonies where there's nothing cool to do. Just before I left, though, I met this real hot dude; his name's J-J, and he looks like—" Cat couldn't finish her description because Hooter's face unexpectedly got in the way, and the sound of his voice when he pleaded, "I'm not asking you to stay for me; stay for yourself, Cat," distracted her.

Cat watched her mother light another cigarette off the end of the preceding one and braced herself when her mother studied her through a thin veil of smoke. Cat narrowed her own gaze and stared back, hard. Something was up, all right; Mom never looked straight at her if she could help it.

"I think it'd be a good idea if you went back there, Cathy," Gwen Kincaid said quietly. "I think you should go back to that farm."

Cat drained her glass of milk. "How come this sudden interest in my welfare?" she demanded. "You've never been able to get *your* act together, so how come you think you've got any right to give me advice about *mine?*"

Cat was pleased to note that at last two bright pink spots appeared on her mother's cheeks. I'm getting to her now, she thought triumphantly, and decided to press her advantage.

"Anybody'd think you were the only Vietnam war widow who ever lived. Listen, more'n fifty-five thousand guys died over there; I read that in history class last year. But the way you've carried on, a person would think you were the only one it left without a husband." Cat paused, took a deep breath, and charged on.

"You never tried to be a regular mother either; you let Gram do it all. She was the one who went to work every day, who came to my school conferences, who got supper every night. Even after she retired from the box factory, she went back and cleaned toilets at night. All you ever did all day was sleep. Or watch TV." Cat leaned across the table toward her mother. "Or drink beer with your boyfriends," she added insolently.

Gwen Kincaid silently inspected her fingernails, which were long and painted a feverish shade of pink. "There's not much I know how to do," she offered by way of excuse. "I don't know anything about whatchamacallems, computers, or stuff like that. Nowadays, a person needs to have, you know, job skills and all. I don't have any of those, Cathy. It always seemed easier just to—" Her small, wistful voice trailed off.

"To have guys coming and going, bringing beer and cigarettes, right? If you didn't have that insurance from my father—" Cat glared at her mother's bent head, noting with grudging surprise that her hair was a pretty medium brown color, the same as her own used to be. Her mother twisted the cord on her robe, but when she spoke again, Cat detected an unfamiliar, stubborn note in that little-girl voice.

"Cathy, let's not argue anymore. All I'm saying, see, is that you've got to go back to that farm. You won't be able to come here anymore."

Cat was stunned. It was one thing to have run off, to have vowed never to return; it was quite different to be told you were no longer welcome even if you'd decided to come back. It was queer, Cat thought later, but at the moment her mother said, "You won't be able to come here anymore," the fierceness of her own jungle heart melted away. Her strength deserted her. She gathered up her breakfast dishes, stood, and propped herself weakly against the sink. Her knees were wobbly; her palms were damp.

"How come?" she asked in a voice so faint that she could barely hear it herself.

"Arnie—see, he didn't know I had a kid—not that he's really got anything against kids—but we've been planning

113

to—" Her mother stopped and started again. "See, I thought maybe with Arnie things'll be okay, that with just the two of us we could—"

"The two of you?" Cat echoed. "You want to get rid of me permanently because of *Arnie*?"

Her mother held up a pink-nailed hand as if to ward off a blow. "I got married so young, Cathy," she murmured defensively. "I was a mother of a tiny baby and then a war widow before I even knew who I was as a person. It was Gram who kept me afloat; she was strong and could do it. You're just like her, Cathy. You're strong; you'll be okay. You know how to take care of yourself. And if I can start all over with Arnie—he'd like to go to California, see; he says there's lots of construction work out there. You'll be okay, Cathy; I know you will."

"It's not me you're thinking about!" Cat yelled. Her strength returned; she felt blood hammer in her wrists, temples, the middle of her chest. "I'm just a souvenir left to you by a guy who died in Vietnam! You probably never wanted a kid; I'm not somebody you ever loved! And how could my dad love me when he got killed even before I was born?" She hoped the neighbors on either side of 272A heard every word.

Gwen Kincaid reached into the pocket of her red robe for another cigarette. Cat set her dishes on the counter and snatched the pack out of her mother's hand. "You light up one more time, and I'm gonna set fire to this place!" she threatened. Instead of grabbing the pack right back, her mother sat meekly, hands locked in her lap, like a child who'd been beaten.

Cat realized suddenly that's what her mother was: a child who'd been beaten. Beaten not by parents or husband or lover but by a life that had been too much for her.

She'd somehow never grown past being that seventeen-year-old girl who'd run away to marry a boy on his way to Vietnam, a boy who never came home to see the child he'd fathered. When her mother glanced up at last, Cat saw how dull her green eyes were and heard how feathery with lost hope her voice was.

"I'm sorry, Cathy," she whispered. "I can't help you. I'm not sure I can even help myself. You'd be better off at that place where the welfare people took you."

The fury and rage that had been recaptured a moment ago drained out of Cat like water out of a leaky bucket. The best part of being angry all the time was that you always felt tough and strong; when you were mad, you had the conviction you could take care of yourself. And if you couldn't do that, you ended up being just like Gwen Kincaid, being beaten by a life that overwhelmed you, right?

"Don't worry about me," Cat declared stonily. She turned and slammed her dishes in the sink so hard that she broke the jelly glass. "Don't sweat about me staying here; I never planned to in the first place." She tore through the living room into her old bedroom, scooped her clothes up, and threw her black jeans and black shirt, along with everything else, into her backpack. She shoveled all her makeup off the top of the commode in the bathroom and dumped it into her purse, bottles and jars and brushes and eyelash curler all in a jumble. When she slung her purse over her shoulder, it felt as if it were weighted with gold bullion.

At the door, Cat turned to her mother, surprised to discover how much taller she was herself. "I'm gonna need some cash," she announced brusquely.

"I figured you would," her mother answered, and

reached into the pocket of her robe. Cat felt numb: her mother had planned the whole thing in advance—the announcement about not being able to stay at the apartment because of good old Arnie, the encouragement about going back to Sweetberry—had been so sure of the outcome of the discussion that she'd stashed money in her pocket earlier this morning.

"This is all I can spare, Cathy, but I want you to promise you won't hitchhike to that farm. This money will be enough to buy you a bus ticket and give you a little bit extra."

Cat stared, momentarily hypnotized, at the green bills in her mother's palm. At the last minute, wasn't her mother going to beg her to stay? Hooter Lewis had said, "Don't go, Cat; don't go." Did he care more about her than Gwen Kincaid did? Her mother said nothing, however, so Cat snatched the bills out of her hand.

"I'm sorry, Cathy," her mother whispered in that small child's voice that Cat despised. "You'll be okay, though; you're like Gram and can do anything you have to do."

Cat clamped her jaws tight. Would it do any good to tell Mom how spooky it'd been last night in the dim yellow light of Davey's hallway? Would her mother be alarmed at how scary it had been to run up behind the Davis car for fear it might be full of young guys looking for a good time? If she told about that night in the park, waking up to find somebody's dog breath in her face and hands that groped at the waistband of her jeans, would Mom reach out finally and exclaim, chagrined by her former indifference, "Oh, Cathy, I never realized—"

When her mother plucked a fresh pack of cigarettes off the coffee table, Cat knew there was nothing she could

116

confess that would elicit the response she needed from Gwen Kincaid. She straightened the bills, rolled them into a tube, and stuck them in the front pocket of her jeans. Never stash cash in a hip pocket; it was a rule she'd learned her first week on the street, when some light-fingered person had relieved her of fifteen bucks. Then Cat looked steadily into her mother's eyes.

"Mrs. Allen keeps telling me I've got this problem. Acting out, that's what she calls it. She says it means I do things just so I won't have to think about my real problems." Cat paused. "Well, lady, I got news for you: you've got problems too. If you were smart, you wouldn't go to California; you'd go downtown to that People's Free Clinic and get yourself a counselor. You need help a lot more'n I do."

Gwen Kincaid hugged herself as if she were cold, and averted her glance. "I'll write to you after me and Arnie get settled," she promised in her mild child's voice.

"Don't bother," Cat said indifferently. She marched out the door and slammed it shut. She didn't look back. She clomped resolutely down the hall, down the stairs, and out to the corner to wait for the B. She rested her thumbs in the belt loops of her second-favorite pair of jeans, the stonewashed ones, and squinted against the noontime glare.

"I'll try the Hideout first," she declared to the empty bus shelter. Something would be going on there; she'd never once gone to the Hideout and found it deserted. Someone down there might be able to give her a line on a good place to crash for a couple days. She'd buy a paper first thing, would check the "Help Wanted" columns till she found a job at a place where she wouldn't be apt to run into any welfare workers. She'd try to stay loose for

117

the rest of the summer; no way, though, did she intend to go back to Sweetberry.

Cat short-cutted across the park, which was empty except for a family with three little kids at one of the picnic tables near the joggers' path. Their van was parked nearby; it had an out-of-state license, which meant the visitors didn't know it was a scuzzy park, favored by druggies and bums and ordinary down-and-outers. Voices floated to her across the worn grass, and some of the words Cat heard made her feel worse than when she'd walked away from the project half an hour ago.

"Come here, sweetie," the father called to his smallest daughter, a tiny thing with canary-yellow braids halfway down her back. "Come to Daddy, sweetie," he crooned again. Cat turned in time to see the child fling herself into her father's arms, her eyes clamped shut with joy when she was caught and tossed in the air.

Come to Daddy. Was it possible to miss someone who'd died even before you were born? Cat wondered. And what should she call that person, never having known him at all? Mr. Kincaid? Michael? Daddy? In the place where her heart ought to have been, Cat felt a hole big enough to drive a truck through. The only time such emptiness got filled up was when a guy wrapped his arms around her and whispered into her hair, "You're special," or "I love you." The cure never lasted long enough, though; soon she'd have to hear the words again, would need to feel the feeling, would have to find a guy and do things with him that later only made her feel used up and sad, not like a leopard at all.

Cat dodged around a clump of pink rhododendrons, jumped over the steel cable that marked off the joggers' path, and side-stepped down the steep bank toward the underside of the Harley Street bridge. She hoped she wouldn't be the only chick at the Hideout today; she always felt better when other girls were around.

Most of all, Cat hoped that that weird character, the one named Duke, had blown town. Nobody knew for sure where he'd come from in the first place. He just showed up one afternoon, older than most the regulars, and different in a way not easy to describe. Angie'd come closest when she'd observed, "That dude's got real crazy eyes," and had speculated that he'd done too many drugs. That was one thing Cat knew you couldn't mess with if you had to take care of yourself; if your brains were fried, you ended up being somebody's victim sooner or later.

She paused before she stepped out of the bright sunlight into the mellow gray gloom of the underside of the bridge. It was like a cave; no grass grew there, only an occasional weed, spindly and yellow because the sun never lighted the area. She checked the fire pit Rambo had dug; it was full of cold ash. Nighttimes, when that pit glowed with embers, were the best of times at the Hideout. Then you could see the lights of the city reflected in the black water, could hear the lapping of the river against its banks. In the dark, you never noticed how many McDonald's cartons had piled up, not to mention the stacks of cans and bottles. Night healed so many things, including holes in a person's heart.

Cat walked up behind the new couch, the one a couple of guys had snatched from the alley behind the Salvation Army store the week before she'd gotten hauled away to Sweetberry. Her feet made no sound in the sand, and only when she got too close to turn away did she realize who was lying on it.

Duke lifted his shaggy head and blinked. "Now if it ain't the little ol' cat lady herself," he greeted her sleepily. Even from four feet away Cat could plainly tell that he hadn't had a bath since spring.

"Hey, man," she murmured noncommittally, "where's everybody at today?"

"Look who's talking. You ain't been around these parts for a long time yourself."

"Been out of town," Cat said carefully, and took a single step backward.

"Like out of town where?" Duke wanted to know, and propped himself up on one elbow. "East Coast? West Coast? Someplace in between?"

"Nothing that cool," Cat admitted. "The welfare farmed me out again. Literally. They stuck me on a farm that raises bees. Kids who live around there are into something called 4-H."

"Sounds real down and dirty," Duke leered. "Was it?"

"Means head, heart, hands, health—not exactly dirty," Cat said, and took a second smaller step backward. "Well, I guess I gotta get moving. Nobody's here that I was looking for, so—"

Duke sat up and stretched as lazily as a dog in the sun. "Hey, it only takes two to party." He grinned. "C'mon over here, leopard lady." He patted the space next to himself. "Duke needs a little company; he's a lonely old tiger himself." Cat didn't budge. "'Member, I'm the dude who named you—I'm the guy who told you you were like a cat in the jungle. Now be a good little kitty and c'mon over here. Be real nice to old Duke," he wheedled.

"It's too hot," Cat objected, and lowered her rear end into a lawn chair with frayed webbing. "You got anything to drink?" she murmured, stalling until she could decide what to do next.

Duke reached under the couch and hauled out a six-pack of Colt 45. "This is all I got, sweet face," he said, pulling the tab on one and passing it to her. "Drink up," he urged. "It'll help put you in the mood." How could a voice be so velvety but so edged with menace at the same time? Cat wondered uneasily.

She took a swig but was careful not to look in Duke's direction. She temporized. "I got an awful lot on my mind these days. My case worker is probably looking for me right this minute. That old biddy aims to stick me in a detention center when she gets her hands on me." Even from this far away Duke smelled like a goat; a person would have to be crazy to get within two feet of him, let alone get naked with him.

"What you need is some nerve medicine," Duke suggested. "Bet I could give little kitty just what she needs." He reached out with a dirty paw.

Cat flew out of the lawn chair and sauntered nonchalantly away to lean against one of the bridge pillars. "Like I told you, man, I've got lots of stuff on my mind," she reminded him. She sucked at her beer, which, being far warmer than the one she'd shared with J-J last night, made her feel sick to her stomach.

If anything happened to her down here, Cat wondered, would anyone hear if she screamed? She peered up the embankment that she'd come down only moments before, hoping she might glimpse that family in the park. The bank was too steep; all she could see was the steel cable that marked off the joggers' path. The sound of midday traffic, lighter than usual, was nevertheless a dull roar, more than loud enough to block out the sound of six shrieking girls.

Duke rose off the couch and slouched toward her. Cat stiffened; she'd never realized how tall he was, not to mention that he must outweigh her by at least a hundred pounds. She shifted from one foot to the other, and realized that being scared out of your wits in broad daylight was almost worse than being scared in the dark.

The roar overhead was relentless; she might as well save her breath, Cat decided; her yells would be totally wasted. Instead, she dropped her nearly full can of beer into the sand at her feet and jumped nimbly behind the bridge pillar.

"Hey, sweet face, now don't you go teasing old Duke," Duke warned ominously. "Duke don't like to have his tail pulled."

Cat peeked around the side of the pillar. "I'm not teasing, okay? I already told you, man, I've got lots of heavy stuff on my mind."

"Me, too, kitty-cat—but you think it ain't teasing, wearing the kind of clothes you always do? 'Member that little ol' black outfit you used to prowl around in, that one with the rose up here?" He patted his chest. "That shirt was two sizes too small, and you knew it, babe." His eyes were close-set and brutal, Cat realized, the way she imagined a wild pig's might be.

"I gotta go now," she insisted.

Duke reached for her, but Cat dodged his grasp. "Why, you little—" he snarled, closing his fists on empty air. The rage in his voice made Cat clearly understand that if he caught her, she'd never be able to pry herself loose.

Fear put steel springs under her feet when she leaped for the embankment six yards away. As she flew past the

122

lawn chair, she tried to snatch up her backpack but missed. Duke's fingers nearly closed on her arm, but he succeeded only in snagging her purse, pulling it off her shoulder.

Cat was almost to the top of the embankment when her feet went out from under her. Duke's fingers closed like iron bands around her left ankle. She dug all ten fingers into the dirt and kicked backward with her right foot as hard as she could.

Cat felt her heel connect and heard a sickening, spongy sound, then a howl of pain. She looked down to see Duke reel backward, both hands over his nose. Blood gushed through his dirty, splayed-out fingers, and his wounded curses turned the air blue. Cat spied her purse lying at his feet. No way did she dare reach back to retrieve it.

Instead, she clawed her way to the top of the bank, then raced down the joggers' path until she came to the pedestrian walkway that crossed the bridge. She didn't stop once, but ran the length of the bridge until she got to the opposite side of the Harley River. The July sun scalded the back of her neck; her armpits were soaked with sweat. Once on the far side of the river, she leaned over the bridge rail and peered across the water to the site she'd just fled from. What would she do if she saw Duke lying over there dead?

What Cat saw, however, was that Duke had staggered to the water's edge and was squatted there, mopping his bloody face. As she watched, he rocked back on his heels and began to paw through her purse. Cat knew what he'd find there—bottles and jars and an eyelash curler. She patted her front pocket; what he wouldn't find was money. He'd have to be satisfied with Summer Storm eye shadow and Egyptian Wine blusher.

Dazed and out of breath, Cat dragged herself up the east end of Harley Street. Sweat trickled down her forehead, its saltiness stinging her eyes. The sun made the pavement glitter; she felt blinded and dizzy. She crossed the street when the light changed to green and plugged fifty cents into the Coke machine in front of Abe and Babe's Cash Rite Now pawnshop. She hunkered down on the curb and took an ice-cold gulp from the can, then counted the money Mom had handed over this morning.

Only thirty bucks. No way was it enough to last more than a couple of days on the street if you counted renting a room and all. Cat took a second mouthful of Coke, gargled, and spit into the gutter. Half a dozen ants appeared from nowhere and commenced to drink. She shielded her eyes from the sun's glare and tried to think.

Jeez! What'd happened to all her old, familiar options? Davey, Floss, Angie, the Hideout—one by one, they'd turned out to be worthless. Although she'd vowed never to go home again, she'd always secretly figured Mom would have taken her back if she wanted to stay; now even that option was gone. Mom must've really been listening to that TV show telling women to be more assertive and had decided getting rid of her own kid ought to be her first choice.

Cat wiped her forehead and noticed that her makeup was turning orange in the heat. Behind her, people walked steadily up and down the street, but she felt as alone as if the world had suddenly been emptied of humanity. "I think maybe you've done a lot of things to yourself, Cat," Hooter had warned. Remembering those words, Cat felt chilled to the bone.

I've finally become what I only pretended to be, Cat realized slowly.

It was no game anymore; she *was* a lone predator, a cold, hard stalker who depended on no one but herself. She'd bloodied a man's face today and might have come close to killing him. She'd resolutely been a thief and a liar when she'd lived with the Wilsons and the Turners. She'd insulted poor, decent Marjorie Davis with a middle-finger gesture that the woman would always remember with pained dismay. She'd gotten even with Hooter Lewis by trying to get it on with J-J. She'd paid off Annie Bowen by leaving Sweetberry without admitting she'd like to eat a holiday dinner by the light of a beeswax candle.

Being human is so hard, Annie had said. Tell me about it, Cat thought wearily, and chugalugged three long swallows of cold Coke. She dug in her jeans for a quarter. She was too tired to make a final choice. Fate would have to decide this next one for her. Tails, she'd call Mrs. Allen and admit that at last she was ready for Ellensburg; heads, she'd buy herself a one-way bus ticket to Sweetberry.

The quarter came up heads.

Cat poured the remainder of her Coke into the gutter and watched as dozens of ants leaped into the brown pool like an army of swimmers determined to cross the English Channel. She got up from the curb and headed west up Harley Street toward the bus station.

11

"I have to get off about twenty miles this side of Channing," Cat told the bus driver when she handed him her ticket.

"We only make regularly scheduled stops," he replied tersely. "We stop at Willmar, Eagan, Kasson, and Channing in that order, kid. We can't stop just any old place a passenger takes a mind to. That ain't how bus companies are run."

"I gotta get off at that railway crossing near Sweetberry Bee Farm," Cat persisted. The driver, whose face was as lined as a road map and whose nose was blistered from a bad sunburn, regarded her more closely. "Yeah, well, I s'pose you can get off there, seeing that federal safety regulations say I hafta stop at rail crossings, no matter whether anybody wants to get off or not." He tore her ticket in half and gave her a critical head-to-toe examination when he handed the stub back.

"I s'pose you're one of them girls who stays with that woman who sells honey, right?"

Cat nodded, relieved that he seemed to be almost interested. "How come you know about that?" she asked.

"Driving a bus on the same route for fourteen years, you can't help but notice things," he rasped. "I've seen girls like you go there, and I've seen 'em leave too. I asked one of 'em once what it was all about. She said that bee lady—can't remember her name now—took in foster kids or something."

"Annie Bowen; her name's Annie Bowen." Repeating the name made Cat feel somehow connected.

"Whatever. Better take a seat now, kid; I can't get rolling till you do."

Cat picked a seat across the aisle from the driver, where she'd have a good view of the highway. He'd said he had to stop at the railway crossing, but just in case he forgot, she wanted to be sitting close enough to tap him on the shoulder and remind him as soon as she saw the glimmer of Annie's yellow roadside sign.

The silence of the bus, with its handful of passengers locked securely in their own private worlds, made the ride to Sweetberry seem a lot more restful than the first one had been with all those nonstop lectures from Mrs. Allen.

Cat pressed the button on the arm of her seat, let the backrest out one notch, and reflected on the disastrous loss of her purse and backpack. The fate of her black jeans and black T-shirt was clear—Duke would haul them up to the Used Goods Galore store and try to peddle them, plus her backpack itself, for a few bucks. She'd stolen the jeans, but had won that shirt fair and square in a shooting gallery at the Roaring 20s carnival a year ago. She'd knocked over all the ducks in a row, could've picked out a five-foot-tall purple rabbit but had chosen the shirt instead.

"It was two sizes too small for you, babe," Duke had reminded her with a leer. True, true, Cat admitted with an inward shrug, and it'd been no accident either. She'd deliberately chosen a size S, knowing how tight it would fit, how well it'd show off her boobs. Worse by far than the loss of that favorite outfit, though, was having to abandon all her makeup.

Cat sighed, dug her money out of her jeans, and counted it again. After paying for the bus ticket, she had ten dollars left; that sure wouldn't buy anything cool to wear, let alone much makeup to take the place of what had been lost under the bridge. She wondered idly if there was a thrift shop in Channing; you could sometimes pick up neat clothes at a place like that. As for the makeup—well, she just might have to walk around with a naked face for a while. Shades of Shirl, the squirrel. Cat grimaced.

She rubbed her fingers across her forehead and was glad she couldn't see how she looked with sweat-streaked makeup that had turned orange. Massaging her eyes, Cat discovered a tender knot between her eyebrows and explored it carefully with a fingertip. A zit! This was unreal; when she washed her face tomorrow morning, there it'd be, a bright red announcement that she wasn't really much different from other girls after all.

Cat closed her eyes. She wished she could've figured out a way to have sneaked back to Sweetberry under the cover of night, just as she'd left it. That way, she would've been able to walk back up that narrow road in the dark, could've crawled through that porch window, and crept into bed as if nothing special had happened. Peaches would've rolled against her, his weight a familiar, comfortable anchor, and in the morning she'd have gone out to eat breakfast with Annie as if her two-day absence had been nothing unusual.

Jeez—what if Annie was real sore, though? What if she had already called Mrs. Allen and said, "Listen, if you ever find that darn kid, don't bother hauling her back here! Nothing worked out; the whole thing was a terrible fit."

Cat laced and unlaced her fingers in her lap. Well, if that had happened, the next stop was Ellensburg for sure. She'd have wasted twenty bucks trying to get back to another place where she wasn't welcome anymore. She'd always figured Mom couldn't make choices, but when she said, "With just the two of us," Cat had revised her opinion. Those words had summed up perfectly the decision Mom had made: it's gonna be just me and Arnie out there in California and you're not included in the deal.

But whether she ended up at Sweetberry or at Ellensburg, her life on the street was definitely over, Cat realized. If Duke ever got word that she was hanging around again, her life wouldn't be worth the price of a Pepsi.

Cat opened her eyes and stared out the dusty green bus window, remembering how, on that first trip to Sweetberry, she'd scared off a sparrow by sticking her tongue on the window of Mrs. Allen's car. I've always been trying to get even with someone, Cat mused, right down to a chirpy bird hanging on a weed stalk. Was that what acting out was all about, that a person just hit out in any old direction, including getting even with sparrows?

Cat let the backrest out a second notch. Now maybe even Annie would write her off as a bad loan. If that happened, Cat decided, she wanted to go to sleep and sleep forever. It would be better if she just died. Everything would be over that way, all the running, the being scared when you ran up behind cars in the dark, the trying so hard to be a leopard woman who really only wanted to be held close to someone's heart and told that she was loved.

When Cat woke two hours later, it was to feel the bus begin to slow, and through the window she could see the roadside sign advertising Home of the Sweetest Taste This Side of Paradise. She had no purse or luggage to gather up, so she stepped groggily into the aisle to wait for the bus to come to a halt. Her lips were dry, and she moistened them with a cottony tongue.

"Listen, thanks for letting me off here," she mumbled to the driver. Thanks wasn't a word she was in the habit of using; it sounded foreign, as if it belonged to someone else's language. She stepped off the bus, and the driver looked down at her.

"Good luck, kid," he called sympathetically. "You sure look like you're gonna need it," he added, then dismissed her with a quick two-fingered salute off the bill of his cap.

No kidding, Cat thought, crossing the railroad tracks and walking slowly up the road between the double rows of pines and poplars that led to the old gardener's bungalow. When she glimpsed its outrageous pinkness through the trees, a reluctant gladness tugged at her heart.

The geraniums in their rickety tubs were as wimpy as

ever, but she could see that the grass had been freshly mowed. She tiptoed to the side door. Peaches wasn't asleep on the step as he'd been that first morning barely two weeks ago. Cat had hoped he might be; his presence might've been a safe way of getting a conversation started with Annie.

Should she knock, Cat debated, or just stride right in as Hooter had done the first time she ever met him? She rapped lightly on the screened door; walking boldly into Annie's kitchen took more confidence than she possessed right now. When no answer came from inside, Cat checked over her shoulder to see if the Jeep was in its stall in the shed. It was, so she knocked harder. Still no answer.

Maybe Annie had gone behind the house to the garden. Cat went around the corner of the bungalow, and sure enough, there was Annie with a spade in her hand, digging a hole in the soft black earth behind the tomato plants. Peaches, snoozing as usual, lay sleeping in a patch of shade on the grass nearby.

"Hey, Annie," Cat called softly. When Annie didn't glance up, she called louder. "Hey, Annie! It's me. I'm back." She hoped that the beekeeper would consider this good news and would welcome her with that familiar wide, white smile, but Cat was shocked when Annie finally looked up. The woman who faced her across the shallow hole in the dark soil was oddly pale and distracted, not the Annie Cat had hoped to see.

"Jeez, what happened to you?" Cat whispered, astonished.

"I guess I might ask the same of you," Annie murmured. How could a person's complexion fade from rich mahogany to pale putty in only two days? Cat wondered.

131

"Listen, I'm sorry I took off like I did," Cat apologized, and the words on her tongue tasted as peculiar as thanks had earlier. "I should've left you a note or something," she admitted, taking a step nearer. "If you've already called Mrs. Allen and told her to come and get me, I wouldn't exactly blame you. It's what I asked for, I guess."

"We can talk about that later," Annie said. "Perhaps you did what you felt you had to do at the time."

Cat shifted from one foot to the other. She had expected to get bawled out and felt a curious sense of neglect that Annie wasn't angry. Peaches slept soundly throughout the conversation, a fact Cat felt compelled to remark on, lacking anything safer to say.

"Wow, old Peach seems really out of it this afternoon," she observed more cheerfully than she felt. "Did you miss me while I was gone, pooch?" she called. The old yellow dog continued to doze soundly; the light breeze riffling the creamy hair on his flank was his only movement.

"You know, I think he did," Annie mused. "He went out to the porch several times, looking for you. I heard him traipsing up and down the hall in the dark, so I finally got up to see what had him so shook up. That's when I discovered your bed hadn't been slept in last night. And then—" Annie didn't go on.

Cat waited. Maybe she'd get chewed out now; actually, she'd feel a lot better if Annie just blew sky high. "And then—?" Cat prompted hopefully. When Annie didn't reply, Cat tried to speculate what Peaches had done next.

"I suppose he finally went back to his old bed under the table, huh? He couldn't hop up on my bed, see; I had to help him every time. I'd sort of prop his front end up, and

132

then give his back end a boost. I guess his legs were just too stiff to make the jump."

Annie nodded and went back to digging. "That's where I found him this morning all right, back in his old bed. He'd slept in that same basket since he was a pup." Cat heard Annie sigh. "I'm just glad"—she sighed again—"that the end for my dear old friend was as peaceful as his whole life was."

Cat studied the dog with a suspicious sideways glance. The breeze continued to riffle the pale yellow hair on his flank. He was sleeping so soundly—maybe *too* soundly? "The end—?" Cat repeated uneasily.

"You must remember that he was quite old," Annie said quietly. "He had his eighteenth birthday last month, which means he was mighty elderly for a dog. So I can't say it was a surprise, but—oh, his going seems to have left such a big hole in my life." She spoke in a quavery, not-really-Annie voice.

Peaches isn't sleeping, Cat admitted unwillingly. Last night, perhaps as she herself stood alone at nearly midnight in the dim yellow light of Davey's hallway, Peaches had died quietly in his old bed under Annie's kitchen table.

Annie leaned on her shovel and began to speak to the treetops beyond Cat. "I suppose the hard part of losing him is that Tuck and I picked him out together."

Tuck? That must be her brother's name, Cat decided.

"I was nearly forty when I was married," Annie continued reflectively, "and Tuck was even older. We decided right away that we wanted to live in the country, and it seemed natural that one of the first things we'd buy together would be a dog to keep us company."

"You were—*married*?" Cat asked incredulously.

"Only for a year," Annie murmured. "I was a widow almost before I got the knack of being a wife. Tuck's death seemed so terrible because it was so ordinary."

Cat stepped lightly across the grass to where Peaches lay and knelt beside him. She laid a cautious hand on his haunch; he was solid and unmoving beneath her touch, and she removed her fingers quickly. "How can anyone's death be ordinary," she whispered, "especially when it's someone you love?" Gram's death hadn't been ordinary, and neither had Michael Kincaid's.

"I ought to have said the reason for his death was ordinary." Annie corrected herself. "We'd gone camping, you see; Peaches was with us, so tiny that we kept him in a cardboard box in the tent at night. Tuck caught what we both thought was the flu, and finally we came home so that he could go to bed and get well."

Annie lowered her gaze from the treetops, and Cat could see the shadow of remembered pain in the beekeeper's hazel eyes. "But Tuck only got worse, not better. It turned out that he had something called encephalitis. It's a disease that can be carried by mosquitoes. He'd been bitten several times, you see, while we camped."

This time Annie's sigh was more like a moan. "If he'd been drowned trying to save somebody's life—or killed in a war—but to die of a little old mosquito bite—well, it just never seemed fair!"

Cat watched silently as the grave in the black earth grew wider and deeper. Once Annie had been just like Mom: she'd been part of a couple, one-half of a pair called Tuck and Annie, just as Mom had been part of a pair called Michael and Gwen. Annie had been in love; she'd found someone who'd thought her straight hair was okay, that the gaps between her square white teeth gave her smile character. Together, Mr. and Mrs. Tuck Bowen had bought themselves a puppy they'd named Peaches.

Annie set her shovel aside, spread a piece of yellowed sheet on the grass beside the dog, then stooped to lift him onto it. Cat jumped up. "He's heavy!" she exclaimed, knowing that he was. "You better let me help you." In death, Peaches seemed to weigh even more than he had in life, but working together, she and Annie managed to transfer the dog onto the sheet, which, rather than being soft and pliable, was stiff and crackled as they folded it around his body.

"It feels and sounds that way because of the wax," Annie murmured. "In olden times, a shroud of wax-soaked linen was wrapped tightly around a body to exclude air; it was what was done before embalming was discovered." Annie made sure that the cloth was folded snugly around the dog.

"Back then it was called a cerecloth," she went on, "*cera* being a Latin word for wax. Such a cloth was also thought to ease one's passage into heaven."

When Annie glanced up, Cat realized that the beekeeper wasn't at all embarrassed by the tears that glistened on her broad, pale cheeks. "Oh, I know it was foolish to have made such a cloth for a dog," she admitted ruefully. "It took me a long time to make it too and was the main reason I didn't get him buried right away this morning. Not only that, I used up all the wax I'd told you we'd save to make candles!"

Cat helped Annie lower Peaches into his final resting place. Annie scooped up a shovelful of soft black earth and sprinkled it gently over the shrouded form in the grave.

135

Cat reached for the shovel herself. "Let me do it too," she whispered.

"Tomorrow I'll go over to the river and get some nice, smooth stones to build a cairn above him." Annie sighed, passing the shovel to Cat. "I don't fancy having raccoons or badgers digging up his bones and disturbing his sleep."

Cat smoothed the last layer of dirt over the grave. "Maybe I could go with you," she offered shyly. "If you want me to, I mean."

"And in the spring, I'll plant some daisies among the stones," Annie added, ignoring the offer.

"That'd look pretty," Cat agreed, and tamped the soil down firmly with the heel of the shovel. What kind of dirt did they have over there in Vietnam? she wondered suddenly. Was it black like this, or sandy like the stuff under the Harley Street bridge, or maybe yellow like the dirt on the road leading from the highway to Annie's house?

"My mom's a widow too," Cat was startled to hear herself blurt out. It was not information she'd shared with anyone for a long time.

"My dad died in Vietnam two months before I was born. He got blown up by a mine; there wasn't enough left of him to even send back home to be buried," she rushed on, as if the words were a burden she'd been carrying too long and suddenly needed to be rid of.

"His name was Michael James Kincaid. He was only nineteen years old; he never knew me and I never knew him, but sometimes I think I've looked in a lot of different places trying to find him."

"That must hurt," Annie observed softly. Cat shook her head vigorously, *no*, but the tears began to come anyway.

"How can you miss a person you never knew?" She sniffled helplessly. What was happening to her? She hadn't cried even when Gram died, hadn't shed a single tear any of the times she'd stalked off from the project—so why now, as she helped someone else bury a pet that she herself had only slept with a few nights under a patchwork quilt?

"Perhaps when we lose someone we love, we go right on missing them no matter how much time goes by," Annie suggested. "That's always how I felt about my Tuck. Oh, it got easier after a while, but somehow the ache never quite went away. For you, I'm sure it's been the same. Your father was your father, whether you had the chance to know him or not."

No, the ache had never gone away, Cat realized, and wiped her nose energetically with the back of her hand. "You never said if you wanted me to go with you to the river to get those stones," she reminded Annie, anxious not to think anymore about Michael James Kincaid. "Or maybe you've already called Mrs. Allen and told her that—"

Annie retrieved the shovel from Cat's grip and touched Cat's hand lightly as she did so. "No, I didn't call any of the welfare people," she assured her. "I figured maybe you deserved to have a couple of days to think over what you'd done."

"Does Hooter know I took off?" Cat asked. She hoped not, but Annie nodded yes. "He cut the grass for me this morning while I made the cerecloth," she replied. "He wanted to know if you were still sleeping, and when I told him you'd flown the coop, the news didn't seem to surprise him very much."

Cat studied the smooth, black oval mound that marked

137

Peaches's grave, then followed Annie around the tomato plants toward the house. "Do you have Hooter's phone number?" she asked casually.

"Yep; it's on that blackboard next to the phone in the kitchen. Upper lefthand corner, I think."

"I've got to call him tomorrow. There's something he's gotta help me do," Cat announced, then hesitated uncertainly. "He might not be real crazy about talking to me, though," she added.

"Why not?"

"You don't know what happened over there," Cat murmured, and hiked her shoulder in the direction of the deserted old house standing in its weedy yard.

"I've got a fairly good idea. Hooter told me a few things this morning."

"Oh." Not knowing exactly what he'd said, Cat decided it was better not to explore the subject further. When Annie turned at the back door, Cat saw that the tracks left by her tears made Annie seem younger. She seemed softer too, like a person who really knew what it meant to have a hole in her heart.

"Cat, I think all of us are a lot like the bees," she said gently. "They need each other and so do we. The difference is, we have to choose our affections, and when everything goes haywire, we have to choose all over again."

Tell me about it! Cat groaned silently. Hadn't she pretended never to need anyone, but hadn't she just the same looked everywhere—under bridges, in scuzzy apartments, in the dark in parks with guys she didn't even really like—for someone who would be the sort of person Michael James Kincaid might have been? She'd searched high and low, pretending to be hard and dangerous, for a

138

person who would be kind and loving and able to stop her from doing dumb things that made her feel more lost and lonesome than ever.

Now, Cat realized, not even Annie Bowen could do that. The only person who could rescue her now was Cathleen Kincaid, daughter of Michael and Gwendolyn.

12

When Cat washed her face the next morning, she discovered that her zit had become a small, hard red dot smack between her eyebrows. She searched Annie's bathroom for something to disguise it, but found only a bottle of inexpensive moisturizing lotion. She smoothed some on her face, noted that it did very little to hide anything, and studied the image of the stranger reflected in the mirror.

Without mascara, eyeliner, or eye shadow her eyes still were green, but in no way were they feline anymore. They seemed round rather than narrow, and nothing in their expression would remind anyone of a dangerous animal lurking in the heart of the jungle.

Could this be the same person who'd stood alone with a sackful of empty bottles in her arms in the dimly lit hallway outside Davey's apartment? Cat wondered. Was this the girl who'd splattered Duke's nose all over his face and left him bleeding on the banks of the Harley River? In order to scrub her face a moment ago, she'd held back her corkscrew curls with a yellow sweatband from one of Annie's bathroom drawers, which only added to the ordinary appearance of the girl who, astonished, stared back at her.

"If Shirl was plain, you're a whole lot plainer!" Cat admitted to the stranger, and couldn't decide whether or not she actually liked what she saw.

As soon as breakfast was over—Annie, thoughtfully, had set out only orange juice and a single slice of dry toast for her—Cat checked the blackboard for Hooter's phone number. Sure enough, it was scribbled in blue chalk in the upper lefthand corner, just as Annie had said it would be. When Cat dialed his number, however, her hand trembled so badly that she had to hang up before the call went through.

She leaned her forehead against the smooth coolness of the blackboard. Jeez, it'd be superhumiliating if he refused to talk to her, just slammed the receiver down the second he heard her voice.

She'd give anything not to have to remember that final night on the porch of the old house, when she and J-J had been illuminated like two characters in a bad play by the headlights of the Green Machine. She must've looked like a real sleazeball, all right, leading J-J into that darkened living room to do exactly what Hooter suspected she intended to do. But without Hooter's help today, Cat knew, there was no way she could carry out the plan that had taken shape in her mind yesterday when she stood beside Annie at Peaches's graveside.

Cat gritted her teeth and dialed a second time. The phone rang twice on the Lewis end of the line, and she was relieved to think the call might have to be temporarily postponed. Then she heard Hooter boom into the

141

receiver, "Lewises!" as heartily as he'd cried, "So how's it going, Anna Banana?" on the morning he'd delivered the Starmaker queen and three pounds of bees to Annie's kitchen.

Cat cleared her throat and was surprised how slippery her grip on the phone had suddenly become. "It's me," she announced in a quivery voice. There was no reply from the other end of the line.

"You know, Miss Runaway USA," she prompted. She was greeted by continued silence.

"So you decided to come back, huh?" Hooter asked when Cat had almost given up hope.

"Must have," she admitted. "I'm talking to you, and this isn't long distance, so it must mean I'm here, right?" She tried to steady her voice and put a light, careless gloss on her next words. "Listen, Hooter, there's something I need to—what I mean is, I need you to do me a favor."

"Sure you do. You want a ride back to the city. Well, forget it. Ditto a trip to Florida."

"It's not that kind of favor," Cat insisted, and lowered her voice to a whisper. "Listen, Hooter, I can't go into detail on the phone because Annie's right in the next room. Meet me over at the old house, though, and I'll explain everything."

"Oh, I bet you will! Just like you explained it to me before. Like you tried to explain it to J-J Irving. Hey, people talk all the time about how guys just want to get it on with girls, that it's always girls who get a raw deal, but all *you* want to do is—"

"This is different," Cat insisted urgently. "Anyway, Hooter, what I need is for you to do me *two* favors," she added.

Hooter whistled shrilly through his teeth. "One thing I

gotta admit, lady—you sure got guts!" Once, Cat would've considered it the highest sort of compliment. Now it didn't sound so great.

"I need to borrow a few bucks."

Hooter whistled again. "So how many is a few?"

"About ten—and I'll pay you back as quick as I can."

"What d'you need it for?" he demanded suspiciously.

"I can't tell you on the phone," Cat hissed. "Meet me at the old house, and I promise I'll explain everything. This is for real, Hooter."

There must've been something in her last words that convinced him, Cat realized, because his next question was, "When? I don't have to work this morning, so I could be there in an hour."

"Great," she whispered. "See you then." She hung up quickly, before he had a change of heart. She heard Annie's footsteps in the hallway, hastily refolded last night's newspaper, and laid it casually on the kitchen table. For this to be the right kind of surprise, Annie must suspect nothing.

Half an hour later, when the breakfast dishes had been done (she washed them before Annie had a chance to suggest it was a good idea), Cat crossed the thistle-bright field that separated the two old houses and, with twenty minutes still to spare, went upstairs to the empty bedroom that overlooked the yard below.

Cat checked her watch, wondering if Hooter would be on time. She studied the handsome gold hands on the black watch face and decided that tomorrow she'd mail it back to the Wilsons. She'd write a letter to go with it; she'd tell them she was sorry to have put the snitch on it from their desk drawer, would thank them for having tried to help her. She wouldn't mention, of course, that

143

she'd almost pawned the watch one day at Abe and Babe's Cash Rite Now shop on Harley Street.

When Hooter coasted his truck into the shade of the oak tree below, Cat retreated a single step from the window. He got out of the Green Machine without a smile, and when he glanced upward, no broad, friendly grin lighted his face. This time Cat left the buttons on her shirt exactly as they were, didn't pinch her cheeks to make them pink or lick her lips to make them shiny. She came slowly down the stairs into the living room just as Hooter came through the front door.

For a moment they scrutinized each other warily, like wrestlers surprised to find themselves in the ring together. "H-H-Hi," Cat murmured, embarrassed by her stutter.

"You look different," Hooter observed coolly.

"I suppose I do," Cat groaned, touching the hard red knot between her eyebrows.

"You used to—well, most girls around here don't wear very much makeup. Sometimes you used to look like—" He mercifully didn't continue. Someday, Cat thought, I'll tell him I intended to look like a leopard, that I wanted to scare people at the same time I wanted them to like me. Hooter shuffled his feet but didn't desert the safety of his post near the open door. Their mutual uneasiness filled the room like the pale, cool stuff Annie pumped out of her smoker.

"So anyway, what'd you want to see me about?" Hooter parried finally.

Cat reached into her hip pocket and took out the newspaper clipping. "I gotta buy a dog," she mumbled.

Hooter was amazed. "A *dog*? What d'you need a dog for?"

144

"It's not for me," Cat answered.

She saw she had succeeded in capturing Hooter's undivided attention. He tilted his head back, his dark eyes wide, and smiled at last. "It's for Annie, right?" Cat nodded. "That's neat! Y'know, she really loved ol' Peaches, and with him gone, she'll sure feel—"

"'Mutt.'" Cat interrupted, reading aloud from the clipping. "'Twenty dollars each. Buyer pays only for shots. Give a good dog a nice home.'" Then she frowned. "It doesn't say if they're puppies, though," she complained. "That's what Peaches was when Annie picked him out, and I figured a pup would be the best kind of—"

"We won't know for sure what kinda dogs they are until we go see 'em," Hooter pointed out matter-of-factly. "We," he'd said, Cat observed with relief.

Instead of heading straight for his truck, however, Hooter continued to slouch against the doorjamb. His gaze searched her face, and he still seemed to have reservations. "This is sure some kind of quick turnaround," he remarked. "Only a couple of nights ago you were all hot to drag J-J in here and peel his clothes off him like he was a candy bar. Now, all of a sudden, you want to go out and buy Annie—"

"It's not as sudden as you think," Cat objected softly. Listen, she'd had plenty of reasons lately to change her mind about a lot of stuff, right? But how could she explain Duke to Hooter, or the things Floss and Angie were doing now? If she tried, he'd end up thinking she was a crummier sleazeball than he did already, and might even reconsider his decision to help her.

The only thing she could admit right now was, "I've pretended to be somebody I wasn't for a long time, Hooter." Then she remembered Annie's words from yesterday afternoon. "But see, people are a lot like bees; they need each other too, which is why I came back to Sweetberry." She hesitated. "It's the reason I'm gonna try to stay here if the welfare'll let me."

Hooter made way for her to saunter past him onto the porch, and Cat was painfully aware of how bright his T-shirt was, how squeaky-clean he smelled. "What's the address of this place we're headed?" Hooter murmured, and lifted the clipping from her fingers, brushing her fingers lightly with his own.

"Oh, yeah, I know where this is," he announced. "The Millers—they've got a kid my sister's age. I think they have something to do with the county humane society."

"But what kind of dog can you get for only twenty bucks?" Cat worried out loud. She remembered passing the Pet Palace next to Woolworth's the day she stole that pink-handled mirror; in that shop, behind a glass wall, she'd seen a gray poodle for sale for three hundred dollars. For twenty bucks what a person got probably would be skinny, mean, and not much to brag about. For sure it wouldn't be a peach.

"Only one way to find out," Hooter declared briskly, now fully committed to helping. "C'mon; we'll go see for ourselves."

Once settled in the cab of the Green Machine, Cat was careful to sit well over on her own side and to loop her arm carelessly out the open window just as Hooter did. The wind tugged at her corkscrew curls, and she found herself wondering how long it would be before her hair once again was the same ordinary brown color that Gwen Kincaid's was.

Hooter began to whistle "You Picked a Fine Time to

146

Leave Me, Lucille" as they flew down the highway, then asked guardedly, "So where'd you go when you took off from Sweetberry, Cat?"

Cat didn't answer right away. "I ended up going to see my mom," she admitted, still a little surprised that she had. "I was lucky with my hitch too; I got a lady and her husband who were really nice." Poor Marjorie Davis; Cat wished there was a way to let her know that rude gesture had been a terrible mistake. "My mom's going to California, though, so I guess I won't be seeing her anymore." She sighed. "She's going with her boyfriend, Arnie. I think she wants to get married again."

Cat cupped her hand to catch some wind, which eluded her grip even as she closed her fingers around it. Just like what's been happening to me lately, she mused; I reach out to hold onto something, but it's hard to capture, just like a mother.

"I went back to some of the places where I used to hang out," she admitted. "There was this apartment where I used to crash a lot; I found out the guy who rented it got hauled off by the cops. I guess he went bonkers or something." Cat could feel Hooter's dark eyes inspect her profile.

"If things work out okay, I won't leave Sweetberry again." She sighed. "I never planned to live on a bee farm, but I guess it's the best place for me to be now. If you'll excuse the pun," she added wryly.

From the tail of her eye, Cat saw Hooter nod and was grateful when he offered no comment. Sometimes, all you wanted to do was just talk, not be advised. "I lost everything I owned while I was gone," she went on. "All my clothes. My purse. Everything except my money, most of which I had to blow on a bus ticket to get back here.

147

That's why I gotta borrow from you now—sorry about that—but I'll get you paid back as quick as I can."

"Don't sweat it," Hooter said easily, and plucked a ten-dollar bill from his wallet on the dash. "Ten bucks won't make or break me, Cat."

"I'm gonna get a job," Cat declared nevertheless, "so you don't need to worry." She was about to inquire if extra help might be needed at that drugstore where Shirl worked when Hooter wheeled into a yard with a neatly manicured lawn that was decorated with a pair of life-sized plastic deer. At the end of the driveway, near a garage, Cat could see a dog kennel with several dogs housed in separate cages. A family stood nearby and obviously had just acquired a pet, for a boy about ten years old had a small spotted dog on a leash and was leading it away to a waiting station wagon.

When Cat told Mr. Miller that she needed a male dog, preferably a puppy, Mr. Miller apologized and told her that he had two males but that neither was a pup. "Both seem to be nice dogs, though," he assured her. "One looks to be mostly spaniel; used to belong to a family over in Channing who moved into a condo where pets aren't allowed. The other is a lord-only-knows-what breed. Want to look at either of 'em?"

Cat nodded and could see right away that the spaniel was a dog that'd been well cared for. He leaped eagerly against the wire of his cage and kiyied shamelessly that he was exactly the pet she was looking for. The dog in the neighboring cage stood uncertainly in the middle of it and made no effort to advertise his worthiness.

He was tall and thin in the chest, Cat noticed, her fingers hooked in the wire of his cage. His legs seemed too long for the rest of him, which was close-coupled, and he steadfastly avoided meeting her glance.

"Looks to me as if he might have some Irish setter in him," Mr. Miller suggested, "if that red color and those soft, droopy ears are reliable clues."

The dog's redness, however, was a faded kind, Cat noted, and his coat needed a lot of brushing. His eyes, as he gazed studiously into the distance, were what held her; they were large and brown and careful. They made no promises and offered no apologies.

"Where'd you get him?" she asked Mr. Miller quietly.

"Didn't get him anywhere, young lady. He just showed up here one afternoon. Maybe some folks just dumped him off along the highway; that happens a lot," he admitted regretfully. "People think, see, that they want a pet, then decide later it's too much trouble to take care of. That's why I run this kennel. The only other thing to do is let animals like these go to the pound, where—if they aren't adopted within thirty days—they're put to sleep."

Mr. Personality, in the next cage, clamored enthusiastically for Cat's attention, but she was riveted in place by the indifference of the scruffy, pale red dog. "Guess he's the one I want," she whispered, and pointed.

"Him?" Mr. Miller seemed surprised. "Why, I never supposed I'd get rid of this chap; I figured he was a candidate for the pound for sure!" He opened the gate of the cage. "You got a leash and collar?" he inquired over his shoulder.

"Here, use this." Hooter stripped his belt out of its loops and handed it to Cat. "It'll do till we get back to Sweetberry." Mr. Miller fastened the belt around the dog's neck and pulled him, still resisting rescue, from the cage. Hooter took the dog while Cat gave Mr. Miller the pair of ten-dollar bills.

"Now, he's had his distemper and parvovirus shots and has been wormed too," Mr. Miller declared, "so he ought to be in good shape." He patted the red dog, who shrank from his touch. "You'll notice, though, that he's a mighty shy pooch. Might take him a few days to warm up to you. Some animals are like that, y'know; you choose them, but it takes them awhile to choose you back. Just let him take his own sweet time, and he'll make you a good pet."

"Oh, he's not for me," Cat said quickly. "He's for a—for a friend of mine." A friend of mine; when, exactly, had she decided that's what Annie was?

In the cab of the Green Machine, the red dog perched nervously on the seat between Cat and Hooter, then began to pant anxiously as the truck wheezed asthmatically toward Sweetberry. "What're you gonna name him?" Hooter wanted to know right away.

"He's Annie's dog," Cat pointed out, "so she's the one who really oughta name him." How should she present him to Annie, though? It didn't seem enough just to haul him in the back door and say, "Here's a pooch for you." She'd really like to do it with more fanfare, Cat decided, and was suddenly inspired.

"Turn in at the old mansion," she commanded. "Then you go over and tell Annie I'm waiting for her over here. Don't tell her why, though."

Hooter wheeled obediently into the shade of the oak tree. "You want me to come back too?" he asked.

Cat glanced away. "I think right now it's gotta be just Annie and me," she answered. "And the dog, of course." She was silent a moment. "But you could come back tomorrow. If you wanted to, I mean."

It was Hooter's turn to be silent. "Maybe I will," he said finally. "If you aren't doing anything, maybe we could go somewhere."

"Maybe we could," Cat agreed, feeling as shy as the red dog sitting on the seat between them. She looped her fingers under the belt collar when she opened the truck door for fear the dog would bolt and disappear even before he'd gotten used to being taken care of again.

"I'll send Annie right over," Hooter promised as Cat led the dog onto the porch of the old house. "Mind if I give Shirl a lift tomorrow?" he added with sly innocence. "I don't think she's got herself a new battery yet."

Cat stared, her cheeks hot. "Gotcha!" Hooter teased, and headed out of the yard toward Annie's bungalow. "This time it'll be just you and me," he called good-naturedly over his shoulder.

Cat led the dog into the living room and shut the door. She sat down on the steps that ascended to the second floor and touched the knot between her eyebrows. It wasn't tender anymore; maybe by tomorrow it'd be almost gone. The dog, Hooter's belt still around its neck, sat down in the middle of the living room, shivered, and regarded her with cautious brown eyes.

"Listen, it's going to be okay," Cat counseled him. Was she speaking to him or to herself? she wondered. "This new life won't be like the one you left behind, whatever that was, but hey, it might be better. Annie's not so bad, once you get used to her." The dog listened attentively, so Cat went on.

"I never expected to end up at Sweetberry myself," she confided, "but sometimes a person just runs out of places to hide, y'know? When I first hit the street, it seemed like a great place to be, but after a while it got to be a lot of work. See, I had to be on the lookout all the time for cops or welfare creeps; I had to rip people off before they ripped me off, and do lots of other stuff."

It was the memory of that other stuff that pained Cat the most—all that reaching for someone in the dark, even in the daylight, hoping always-always-always to fill up the hole in her heart.

In the sunlight that slanted through the beveled glass in the door, the color of the dog that sat in the middle of the room was enriched and deepened. He was almost the color of a dish of raspberry sherbet.

"You may not be much of a peach," she told him, "but you might pass for a raspberry all right." She paused. "Hey, Raspberry," she called tentatively. The dog didn't budge, but inspected her with wary, uncommitted dark eyes.

"Yeah, I know exactly how you feel," she assured him. "It can be real spooky, letting yourself feel safe again. Take it from Miss Runaway USA, it won't come easy." Through the door behind him, Cat could see Annie hurrying, elbows flapping, through the thistle-dotted field.

None of what was destined to come next would be simple, Cat admitted privately. If getting used to Jefferson had been the pits, starting school in Channing might make it look like a picnic. For one thing, sooner or later she was bound to run into J-J Irving again, not to mention that little squirrel, Shirl. If either one of those jerks had a big mouth (and she'd bet her life the one with yellow hair did), then she'd have to deal all over again with that reputation thing, just as she'd had to deal with it after her locker got sprayed with red paint.

Cat heard Annie's footsteps on the porch. And for the rest of the summer, Cat reminded herself, she'd have to spend more time in a hot, sweaty bee suit than she wanted to. Annie would get on her nerves, talking too much about that Starmaker queen, and as if all that weren't bad enough, there'd be times at night in the bed on the porch when she'd think: jeez, I don't belong out here in the boonies, and I never will.

But this time I won't run, Cat promised herself. When morning comes, I'll still be here, and on the next morning, and the one after that too.

Annie opened the front door, her widening smile showing the homely but nice gaps between her teeth. Someday, Cat speculated, I might ask her to call me Cathleen. On that first day at Sweetberry, Cat remembered ruefully, she'd refused to extend her hand for Annie's handshake. Now, she reached out to pull Annie by the shirtsleeve to where the red dog shuddered in the middle of the room.

"Like I told Hooter, he's gonna be your dog, so it's up to you to pick out a name for him. But do you know what I think?" Cat felt a quirky, new lightness of being percolate up from somewhere deep inside herself.

"I think maybe when he was a puppy, he might've been almost as pretty as a dish of raspberry sherbet."